THE VENGEANCE OF THE WITCH FINDER

THE VENGEANCE OF THE WITCH FINDER

JOHN BELLAIRS
By BRAD STRICKLAND

Piccadilly
PRESS

First published in Great Britain in 2019 by
Piccadilly Press
80-81 Wimpole St, London W1G 9RE
www.piccadillypress.co.uk

First published in the United States of America
by Dial Books for Young Readers, 1993

A CIP catalogue record for this book
is available from the British Library.

ISBN: 978-1-84812-818-7
Also available as an ebook

1 3 5 7 9 10 8 6 4 2

Typeset in Sabon LT Std by
Palimpsest Book Production Limited, Falkirk, Stirlingshire

Printed and bound by Clays Ltd, Elcograf S.p.A.

Piccadilly Press is an imprint of Bonnier Books UK
www.bonnierbooks.co.uk

*To Richard Curtis,
adviser and friend*
B.S.

CHAPTER ONE

The young, blue-eyed police officer blinked in surprise. Then he smiled and saluted, touching the narrow brim of his bobby's helmet with respect. "*Good* morning, Mr Holmes," he said in a loud and cheerful voice. "It's wonderful to see you back in London, sir, if you don't mind my saying so."

Lewis Barnavelt could feel himself blushing. A chubby boy of about thirteen, Lewis stood with his uncle Jonathan on the pavement of a bustling London street. Lewis suddenly felt very silly in his blue jacket, brown corduroy trousers, and checked deerstalker hat. "Uh," he mumbled, "I'm not *really* Sherlock Holmes." As soon as he had said it, he felt twice as foolish as before.

The bobby pretended astonishment. "No? Why, I apologise, then. You must forgive me, sir. I simply assumed that you were the great detective travelling incognito. You see, Mr Holmes *was* a master of disguise."

"I know," said Lewis. "We're looking for Baker Street, where he and Dr Watson lived. This is my uncle, Jonathan Barnavelt, and I'm Lewis Barnavelt. We're from America."

"And I am Police Constable Henry Dwiggins. I am happy to meet you both. Good morning to you, sir," said the bobby. He gave Uncle Jonathan an amiable nod.

Jonathan did not notice. He was trying heroically to refold a street map of the city. "Hello, yourself," he said in a grumpy voice. Though no one could tell just by looking at him, Jonathan Barnavelt was a wizard. Not a wicked sorcerer, but a gentle, bearded, heavy set, easy going magician who could conjure up wonderful three-dimensional illusions. Unfortunately, he could not conjure up the ability to read a map well—or to refold it neatly. "We're lost," he confessed to the young policeman. "And my sense of direction has deserted me. Could you please help us find Baker Street?"

The constable smiled. "Of course, sir. A good many Yanks come looking for Mr Holmes's flat, and I have pointed them in the right direction. I like Americans, have ever since I was a young lad. As it happens, I am off duty now. I'll show you the way, if you wish."

"Thank you very much." Jonathan's unsuccessful but athletic efforts to fold the map made his red hair and bushy red beard bristle. A light breeze caught the fluttering paper and napped a corner of it into Jonathan's mouth. "*Ptui!*" he spat. At last he gave up. He simply crushed the map into a more-or-less flat rectangle, which he thrust into the back pocket of his khaki trousers. He wore brown walking shoes, a red vest over a blue open-collared shirt, and a rumpled grey-tweed jacket. "You are most kind," Jonathan boomed, sounding much more friendly now that the map was out of the way. "Of course, Lewis and I know that Sherlock Holmes and Dr Watson were just fictional characters, but we thought it would be fun to explore their neighbourhood."

The officer's eyes twinkled. "Of course, sir. But come to that, fictional characters of that sort are a bit realer than you and me, if you take my meaning. I mean, look at me, now: in a hundred years, who'll come looking for my house? Nobody. But you can be sure that people will still be searching for Mr Holmes's flat at 221B Baker Street. Now if that isn't being real, I don't know what is."

"Could you please tell us where Sherlock Holmes, uh, *might* have lived?" asked Lewis. He normally was timid in the presence of strangers, but he sensed that the young policeman shared his enthusiasm for the Sherlock Holmes tales.

"Well, I have an idea or two." Constable

Dwiggins nodded twice. "If I'm right, he lived rather close by. Come along with me, and you may see what I mean. You have to understand, though, that these old streets have suffered through a lot of changes. Over the years they have been renumbered and bombed and built back up and renumbered again, so your guess may be quite as good as mine."

The three strolled along. It was a cloudy, cool morning in the summer. This was the third day of a six-week European holiday that Lewis and his uncle were taking. Originally, they had planned for Uncle Jonathan's neighbour and best friend, Mrs Florence Zimmermann, to join them, together with Lewis's friend Rose Rita Pottinger. Then Rose Rita had broken her ankle. She could not go on the trip because she would have to wear a cast for about six weeks. Mrs Zimmermann had considerately decided to stay home in New Zebedee to keep Rose Rita company.

Though Lewis missed both Mrs Zimmermann and Rose Rita, he had to admit that even without them, the trip had been—well, maybe the best word was *exciting*. Jonathan and Lewis had travelled by bus and train from New Zebedee to New York. From there they had flown in an aeroplane to London. Lewis had fretted the whole way. What if one of the aeroplane's engines stopped working halfway across the Atlantic? What if fog covered the airport when they arrived, and the pilot crashed the plane into the ground? What if the crazy British traffic, which all moved on the wrong side of the street, got them into a dreadful car accident? Of course, none of these awful events had happened, but Lewis was a worrywart and could not help dreaming up possible disasters. At least he always got a pleasant feeling of relief when his worst fears failed to come true. On Monday Lewis and his uncle had arrived safe and sound at their London hotel. They had spent one day resting, and today they were out to see the sights.

"Now," said Constable Dwiggins suddenly, as he came to a halt at a street corner. "Here we are on Baker Street. Look around, Lewis, and see what you can observe. I've no doubt you know Holmes's methods."

Lewis did as he suggested. On both sides of the street stood rows of three-storey buildings, stone fronted and respectable. At first nothing appeared unusual about any of them. Then Lewis's eyes narrowed. "It must be *that* one," he said. He pointed to the first floor of an apartment building on his side of the street, nestled between the offices of a dairy and a driving school.

"Wonderful, Mr Holmes!" the policeman said with a warm chuckle. "My thoughts exactly. You see the reason, of course."

Lewis thought carefully. "I can see at least three different reasons," he replied at last. "Bravo."

Uncle Jonathan laughed. "Well, I must be about as dense as Dr Watson. I don't see anything about this building that makes it any different from the others. If it isn't too much trouble, would you please tell me what I am missing?"

With a broad smile, Constable Dwiggins nodded to Lewis and asked, "Would you care to enlighten the gentleman, Mr Holmes?"

Lewis put his hands behind his back, the way Sherlock Holmes often did in the stories when he began to explain his deductions. "First," he said, "that apartment house faces east. In 'The Adventure of the Dancing Men' Holmes held a paper up so the sunlight fell upon it, and that was in the morning. That means the windows of Holmes's flat had to look out to the east."

"First-rate," said Dwiggins. "Go on."

A small but noisy truck rumbled by, giving Lewis a chance to think about his next point. When the clamour died down, Lewis said, "You will notice the front door of this building has a semicircular fanlight over it. So did the door of 221B. Watson mentions that detail in 'The Adventure of the Blue Carbuncle.'"

Jonathan shook his head, making his beard waggle. "How on earth do you remember all that?" he asked. "I've read all of Conan Doyle's stories myself, but—oh, well. What is the third reason, my dear fellow?"

Lewis turned and pointed across the street. "In 'The Adventure of the Empty House' Watson says an empty building was directly across Baker Street from 221B. This is the only house that has another one *directly* opposite it. The others are sort of off-centre."

"Right you are!" said Dwiggins. "Good work, Mr Holmes."

"Have I missed anything?" asked Lewis, unable to keep from grinning broadly.

Constable Dwiggins returned his grin. "Oh, one or two minor items, but I can't fault you for them. For instance, I have learned that this is the only house in this part of Baker Street that has a backyard where the famous plane tree could grow. And I happen to know that the stairway has exactly seventeen steps leading up to the first floor. Sorry, you Yanks call that the second floor, I believe. Now, it's true that the flat does not sport a bow window. However, Colonel Moran must have smashed the original window when he fired his airgun through it—either that, or the bombs shattered it during the war. Either way, the present owners must have replaced the broken bow window with a regular window—"

Jonathan raised his hands in surrender. "I give up!" he said. "Take me away. Plane trees and bow windows and seventeen steps mean less than nothing to me, but then I'm as thick as a London fog and as blind as an American bat."

Both Constable Dwiggins and Lewis laughed. "Not at all, sir," said Dwiggins. "And I apologise if you feel left out by all this. It takes a real Sherlock Holmes fanatic to understand the excitement of tracking down the exact location of 221B Baker Street."

Constable Dwiggins had to go then, but before he left, he gave Lewis and Jonathan several helpful hints about what to see in London. Then he and Lewis exchanged addresses, so they could write to each other about Sherlock Holmes. Lewis felt a little sad after the young police officer had gone. It was fine to pretend to be as dashing and as brilliant as Sherlock Holmes. Unfortunately, when he stopped pretending, Lewis had to admit that he was not like him at all. His friends at school often made fun of him because he was fat and something of a bookworm. In fact, Lewis thought, he resembled the "middle-sized, strongly-built" Dr Watson more than he did the tall, athletic Sherlock Holmes. Still, it was fun to assume the role of Holmes, as he had just done. At such times even one or two gloomy thoughts could not completely ruin his good mood.

Lewis and Jonathan went on from Baker Street to visit the British Museum. After that they dropped into some strange little shops in narrow back streets, where Jonathan browsed among musty, cluttered shelves. He was searching for some mystical-looking talisman to give to Mrs Zimmermann as a present. Years before, Mrs Zimmermann had specialised in studying the magic of talismans at the University of Gottingen in Germany. She collected all sorts of mysterious knick-knacks. Jonathan eventually found a small stone scarab that dated all the way back to ancient Egypt. It was an elaborate little carving, a realistic beetle with some flecks of blue and black enamel still showing on its wings and legs. After some bickering with the shop owner over the price, Jonathan bought it. Outside the shop, he held it up and said to Lewis, "According to the shopkeeper, this little doohickey is about three thousand years old. I think Mrs Z. ought to like it, don't you?"

"Sure," said Lewis. "I bet she doesn't have anything like that in her collection."

"I know she hasn't," replied Jonathan. He put the scarab back into its little box. Then he sighed. "Of course, it isn't what I would *really* like to give her."

Lewis knew what his uncle meant. Mrs Zimmermann had once been a much more powerful magician than Jonathan Barnavelt. Jonathan could only create illusions, but Mrs Zimmermann could actually work magical transformations. At least, she could until she had lost her witchy powers in a fight with an evil spirit. She had saved Lewis's life in that battle, and she always said that she had no regrets. Still, both Jonathan and Lewis suspected that she missed her magic more than she admitted. If Jonathan had been able, he would have given Mrs Zimmermann a very special present. He would return her lost magical talents to her. But he could not find a way to do that. Now both Jonathan and Lewis felt a little sad, so they went back to their hotel, planned the next day's tour, and turned in early.

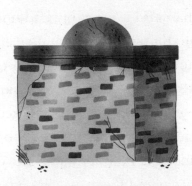

CHAPTER TWO

In all, Lewis and his uncle spent three exhausting but enjoyable days shopping and seeing the sights. They visited the Tower of London, that ancient brooding fortress on the River Thames where in the old days prisoners had lost their heads to the executioner's axe. Lewis was interested to learn that when Henry VIII had had his wife Anne Boleyn beheaded, he had ordered something special: the headsman had used a fine French sword instead of an ordinary axe. Lewis wondered if that had made much difference to poor Anne, and Jonathan said it probably had not, but then it was the thought that counted. They saw Buckingham Palace, where the King of England lived, and they watched the ceremony of the Changing of the Guard. They explored the busy, bustling, and mysterious old city of London, finding something new at every street corner and down every narrow alley. Uncle Jonathan enjoyed himself as long as he could poke about in bookshops and curiosity shops, and soon his normal good humour returned.

Everything went very smoothly, and to his surprise Lewis found himself walking miles every day with enthusiasm. Usually he did not much care for exercise, because he thought of himself as clumsy and heavy, but now these long strolls just gave him more energy. He did occasionally complain about the English food, which he considered bland and odd tasting, but he kept so busy that he hardly thought about that except at mealtimes.

Finally, Lewis and Jonathan checked out of their Mayfair hotel and caught a train to the village of Dinsdale down in Sussex, the countryside well to the south and west of London. "Why are we going to Dinsdale?" Lewis asked his uncle for the tenth or twelfth time that day. Jonathan had been very secretive about this part of the trip, and had announced their destination only that morning.

"Well, I suppose it's time to spring my surprise," said Jonathan, leaning back in his seat. They had a first-class compartment all to themselves and sat facing each other. Jonathan put his thumbs into his vest pockets, as he often did while talking, and said, "I don't know if your father ever mentioned it, Lewis, but our family has a long history. A good part of that history took place here in England."

Lewis's father and mother had both died several years before in a car accident. Ever since, Lewis had lived with his uncle in New Zebedee. In a way, he had become used to his parents' being gone. Still, it always hurt when something or someone suddenly reminded Lewis of his mum and dad. "Uh, no, he never mentioned it," Lewis said in a low voice, trying not to look upset.

Jonathan appeared not to notice Lewis's discomfort. Gazing out the window, he said, "I'm not surprised. Charlie was an optimist, always looking ahead. The past never interested him much. Still, it is true that we have English roots. On your grandmother's side of the family we are Dutch. She was a van Olden before she met your grandfather. I don't know what the Barnavelts were back in the very old days—that name sounds Germanic to me, but I've never researched it. However, for ages and ages the Barnavelts lived in England. In fact, one of our ancestors came across the English Channel with William the Conqueror in the year 1066. Many of our later forefathers were knights serving British kings. My great-great-great-grandfather, Tobias Barnavelt, was the younger son of one of those Sir Something-or-Other Barnavelts. Since Tobias's father willed everything to the older brother, Great-Great-Great-Grandpa Tobias emigrated to America, way back in 1795.

He landed in Boston, where he founded our branch of the family. Eventually his son moved his family west, to New Zebedee."

The train was out of the city now, and it picked up speed as it passed lush woods and green fields. "I still don't know what all that has to do with where we're going," said Lewis.

"Ah. I'm getting to that. The British branch of the family has a manor house in West Sussex, not very far from Dinsdale village. That is where we are going—to visit our umpteenth cousin, who-knows-how-many times removed. His name is Arthur Pelham Barnavelt. He got to know your father back during the war, when Charlie was in the Army Air Corps and was stationed at an airfield not far from Dinsdale. Now Cousin Pelham is eager to meet us."

"And he lives in a real manor house?" Lewis asked, his tone excited. "You mean one like Baskerville Hall, in *The Hound of the Baskervilles*?"

"Right," said Jonathan with a smile and a nod. "Only the name of this one is Barnavelt Manor.

We're going to spend tonight and tomorrow there, getting to know Cousin Pelham." Jonathan paused, his expression thoughtful. After a moment he added, "I don't want to give you the wrong impression, Lewis. It's true that Cousin Pelham is the owner of a genuine manor house. Unfortunately, he is not rich. The British branch of the family suffered financial losses and taxes are extremely high right now. Very little remains of Cousin Pelham's family fortune, except the estate and a modest income. What I am trying to say is that we will have to be tactful."

"Sure," said Lewis. "Only why can't we, well, help out with the expenses?"

Jonathan smiled. "We will, as much as we can without hurting Cousin Pelham's pride." He tapped a bulky, brown-paper-wrapped parcel that they had brought all the way from New York. Lewis knew it contained two tinned hams, a package of sugar, containers of coffee and tea and cocoa, and other goodies. "For instance, I know that Cousin Pelly won't mind us bringing him a CARE package. But remember, in British eyes we are American upstarts—even if I did inherit a pile of money from my grandfather. I've been writing to Pelham for some years, and I've sort of got to know him. I am sure he would resent anything that seriously smacked of charity."

Lewis said he understood. The ride took a long time, but at last the train jolted and hissed to a halt at a small station in the country village of Dinsdale. Jonathan and Lewis got off the train and collected their suitcases. For a few minutes they stood there on the platform, and then an Austin Seven, a tiny, black, old-fashioned open-top car, came chugging and backfiring along. It creaked to a halt, and a spidery man sprang out. His hair was a silvery explosion, his face was lean and long, and his body was all elbows and knees. He wore dark-grey tweed trousers and a rather shabby jacket with leather patches on the elbows, and he sported a bright-red tie.

The second he saw Jonathan, the man's pale-grey eyes lit up. "Cousin!" he called in a crickety voice. "I say, Cousin Jonathan! You're just like a larger, expanded edition of your younger brother, with a beard added. I'd know you anywhere. Welcome! And you must be young Lewis. Come along, come along! We'll nip right out to the Manor and give you something to nibble on. I'm sure Mrs Goodring—she's my housekeeper, quite a treasure—will have something delicious." He helped them load their bags into the cramped car, which proved to be something like assembling a jigsaw puzzle. They got in, making the boxy little car groan on its springs. Finally Cousin Pelham climbed back behind the steering wheel, which was on the right side rather than the left. "All set? Hold on! Here we go!"

The poor old car strained its engine and chugged away from the station at fifteen miles an hour. "Tell me if I go too fast for you," said Pelham in an anxious tone. Lewis could hardly feel a breeze, even in the open car, but Pelham Barnavelt seemed to think they were barrelling right along. Lewis liked this distant cousin at once. The lean old man spoke and moved more like a boy than an adult, and his cheery enthusiasm was infectious. For a while they puttered along a narrow road between hilly, green pastures dotted white with grazing sheep. Then they turned into a long, winding drive. "Here we are," said Pelham. He nodded towards a tiny brick cottage. "That used to be the gatekeeper's house, when we had someone to keep the gate. And now, just around this turn is my ancestral home, and yours as well. Jonathan and Lewis, welcome to Barnavelt Manor!"

The car rounded an overgrown, untidy mass of hedges, and Lewis gasped.

Ahead of them sprawled a huge, grey stone house with leaded windows, two turrets, what seemed a dozen bay windows, numerous gables, and intricate, steeply pitched roofs shingled with shiny black slate. The late-morning sun shone on the old house, and yet its dark, gloomy walls gave the dismal impression of being in deep shade.

It looks evil, Lewis thought. He immediately wondered why the notion had come to him. After all, as Cousin Pelham had said, it was his ancestral home. And surely Sherlock Holmes would scoff at the very idea of a baleful haunted house. He was just being a worrywart again. And yet—

Too much of the house was obviously empty. Too many windows stared out at the world with the hollow expression of a skull's vacant eye sockets. Within a curving drive the grass lay neatly trimmed, but outside that border the lawn and hedges had grown rank and thick. On the tallest chimney perched a gaunt black bird, a rook, with hunched shoulders and lowered head. Everything had a distinct and oppressive air of decay and decline. The house almost looked as if it were giving them a fleshless, threatening grin of sinister welcome.

Lewis felt his heart sink. Cousin Pelham was chattering away. Uncle Jonathan was smiling and relaxed. Neither of them appeared to notice anything unusual. And yet, Lewis thought again, *it looks so evil.*

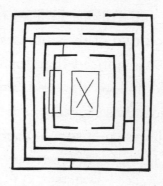

CHAPTER THREE

The antique car wheezed to a halt on a curving drive just before the main entrance of the Manor. Cousin Pelham clambered out. The tall front doors of the manor house swung open, and an old man slowly emerged from within. He was somewhat stout, almost completely bald, and a little stooped, and he wore a rusty-looking black suit. "There's Jenkins," said Pelham. "My man of all work. I say, Jenkins, give our guests a hand with their bags, there's a good fellow."

25

"Yes, sir," said Jenkins in a sorrowful, slow voice. He took two of the suitcases from Uncle Jonathan. Lewis noticed that Jonathan kindly gave the old fellow the two smallest ones. Jonathan and Lewis lugged one heavy suitcase apiece, and Jonathan also managed to hold the parcel of food under his free arm.

"This way, sirs," Jenkins said. He tottered inside the house, and Jonathan followed. Lewis swallowed hard and started into the gloom after him. From behind, Cousin Pelham called cheerfully, "I'll just put the car away. I'll be right in."

Dark wood panelling made the entry hall dusky and cool. Jenkins turned right, and Jonathan and Lewis followed him down a long hall, past six or eight closed doors. Jenkins led them up a stairway to the first floor. Then he turned to the left and down another hall. He set one of the small suitcases down to open a door. "This will be your room, sir," he said to Jonathan. "And young Master Barnavelt will have the one adjoining."

Lewis breathed easier when he saw his room. It was light and airy, with waist-high oak wainscotting and, above that, faded but cheerful wallpaper in pale-blue and white stripes. Two tall, narrow windows spilled sunlight across a worn dark-blue carpet. A quilted sky-blue bedspread covered the sturdy bed. Best of all, the wall at the foot of the bed had a stone fireplace dominating it, and above the mantle was a shield with two crossed swords beneath it. A tall oak wardrobe, an oak desk and chair, and a squat chest of drawers made of the same wood completed the furnishings. Lewis set his suitcase down and sighed in relief. He went to the window and gazed out. He could see the curving drive here too. He realised that it was circular and went all the way around the house. On the far side of the drive a grove of enormous old trees spread their leaves in the sun. When Lewis pressed his face close to the window, he could just make out a vegetable garden with a shed off to his left, behind the Manor.

"Well," boomed Jonathan from behind him, "how do you like it?"

"Oh boy!" said Lewis, pretending more enthusiasm than he felt. "It's like being in a real castle, Uncle Jonathan. Could I take down the swords?"

Jonathan laughed. "Maybe you'd better wait and ask Cousin Pelham about that. He's put the car away and is waiting downstairs to introduce us to the rest of the household. Come with me."

Still carrying the package of food, Jonathan led Lewis down to a small dining room, where a table bore tea, cups and saucers, and a platter of little sandwiches and what looked like biscuits. A plump, red-haired woman in a dark dress and a white apron waited there. At her elbow stood a boy of about twelve who was even fatter than Lewis. He had red hair and wore a red sweater, dark-blue trousers, and a pair of round, steel-rimmed sunglasses. The lenses were so darkly green that Lewis could not even see the boy's eyes. Cousin Pelham came into the room, rubbing his hands together. "Ah, here we all are. Gentlemen, this is Mrs Goodring, my excellent cook and housekeeper, and her son, Bertram. Mrs Goodring, these are our guests, my American cousins, Mr Jonathan Barnavelt and Master Lewis. Shake hands with Lewis, Bertie."

Lewis put his hand out. Bertie did the same. But Bertie held out his hand far off to Lewis's left. Lewis realised with a shock that Bertie was blind. He quickly grabbed Bertie's hand and gave it one brief shake. "Pleased to meet you," said Bertie. "Are there Apaches where you live?"

"Uh, no," said Lewis.

"Oh." Bertie sounded a little disappointed. He added, "Any cowboys, then?"

"No cowboys, either," replied Lewis. "We're from Michigan."

"Oh. What do they have in Michigan?"

"Well, farmers and mechanics and—and just people," said Lewis.

Cousin Pelham had busied himself pouring tea. "Splendid, splendid. You two will get on famously. But let the travellers have a spot of refreshment now, Bertie, and then the two of you can dash along, what?"

"Of course, sir," said Mrs Goodring. "Will you need anything else, Mr Barnavelt?"

"Perhaps Mrs Goodring would like to see what we've brought you," Jonathan said, setting the parcel down.

"Oh, I say," protested Cousin Pelham. "Really, you shouldn't have—but as long as you did, let's have a quick look, eh?" He rubbed his hands together and ripped the paper off the parcel with the air of a six-year-old on Christmas morning. Everyone "oohed" and "aahed" at the contents of the package, and Cousin Pelham positively beamed when he saw the tea. "Absolutely first-rate!" he pronounced. "This is too kind of you, cousin, but I shan't say it isn't welcome! Thank you very much indeed. Mrs Goodring, perhaps you will be so kind as to take these splendid morsels to the kitchen."

"Yes, sir," said Mrs Goodring with a broad,

indulgent smile. "And do you have anything else for me to do, then?"

"No, no, not at all, thank you, Mrs Goodring."

Mrs Goodring put her hand on Bertie's shoulder and turned him towards the door. "Bye, Lewis," said Bertie.

"I'll see you later," said Lewis, and then he blushed. Would Bertie be upset or offended by his saying the word *see*? To his relief the blind boy did not react as he and his mother left the room, Mrs Goodring bearing the box of food before her as if she were carrying the Holy Grail.

"Bit early for lunch, but we'll call this elevenses, what?" Cousin Pelham said. "Here you are, Lewis. Try the scones. Mrs Goodring is wonderful at making them."

The scones were good—toasty and warm and served with jam. For a few moments Pelham and Jonathan chatted about other members of the family. When the conversation lagged, Lewis gathered his courage and said, "Cousin Pelham—"

"Eh?" said Pelham. "Oh, dear me, please don't call me Pelham. Nobody does, you know. I've been Pelly to everyone for nearly seventy years. Sounds much more friendly, don't you know?" His long face folded itself into a smile.

Lewis could not help smiling back. "Uh, Pelly, what is wrong with Bertie's eyes?" he asked.

Pelly's face took on a sad expression. "Ah. Terrible thing, that. It happened in the last months of the war, when he was just a little chap. One of those dreadful rockets exploded close to where he was living with his mother. Mrs Goodring escaped uninjured, but Bertie lost his eyesight. And not long after that his father died in combat. Now, Bertie's grandfather had once worked for my father, so when I learned what had happened, I took on Mrs Goodring as my housekeeper. And a treasure she has been, I must say."

Lewis swallowed. He knew how tragic it was to lose your father.

In a quiet, serious voice, Jonathan asked, "Can't anything be done for him, Pelly?"

Cousin Pelly sighed. "Well, the doctors don't hold out much hope. I'm afraid Bertie has almost resigned himself to a life of blindness. But he's a splendid little chap. I'm sure you and he will get along, Lewis."

"Sure," said Lewis. He felt ashamed of himself. He had been worrying about how gloomy Barnavelt Manor looked from the outside. Now he realised that the house's appearance had deceived him. The people inside the Manor— warm-hearted Cousin Pelly, motherly Mrs Goodring, friendly Bertie, and even helpful old Jenkins—kept it from being as desolate as it looked. If he were really as keen as Sherlock Holmes, Lewis thought, he would have seen past the misleading appearance of the house.

Cousin Pelly rambled on while they demolished the sandwiches and scones. He told Lewis and Jonathan that he had closed off most of the Manor. "Dreadfully expensive to run the whole house, you know," he explained. He and the two servants lived in this small wing. "But if you want to explore the old pile, Lewis, go right ahead," said Pelly. "Bertie knows his way about, and I'm sure he'll be pleased to guide you."

Lewis was happy enough to leave Pelly and Jonathan, who had begun a discussion of Lewis's two aunts. He followed Pelly's directions and found Bertie sitting in a kitchen chair while his mother busied herself washing dishes. "Hello," said Lewis in a timid voice. "Can we play now?"

"Mum?" asked Bertie.

"Go ahead, love. Mind you be careful."

"We will, Mum," said Bertie cheerfully. He slipped out of the chair. "What do you want to do, Lewis?" he asked.

"Well, I'd like to—I mean, could we sort of tour around the Manor?"

"Sure," said Bertie. "I can show you lots of things."

They spent some time exploring the closed-off part of the house. Lewis especially liked the library, where dust covers shrouded the table and chairs and thousands of old books stood in ceiling-to-floor shelves lining three of the walls. Windows filled almost all of the fourth wall, giving a view of gently rolling green hills. "This is Master Martin's study," Bertie explained.

"Who's Master Martin?" asked Lewis.

"Oh, he's been dead for ages," replied Bertie. "Back in the days of the Civil War Martin Barnavelt was quite famous. People said he was a witch."

Lewis blinked. "A witch?"

"Yes. In fact, they took this house away from him for the longest time. He had to defend himself against charges of witchcraft, and even then the Roundheads took over the Manor. Later he had still more trouble getting the house back after the Restoration, but he finally did in 1668."

Lewis had not realised at first that Bertie was talking about the English Civil War. He had read books about British history, and he knew that in 1642 a group of British Puritans had risen up against King Charles I. People called the Puritans "Roundheads" because of the way they cut their hair. Eventually, the Roundheads won the war and beheaded the King. Then for some time the Roundheads ruled England, under Oliver Cromwell. After Cromwell's death the English people restored the monarchy in 1660. It felt sort of weird to be standing in the library of a man who had been involved in a war nearly three hundred years earlier.

"Was Martin Barnavelt really a witch?" asked Lewis.

Bertie laughed. "Don't be silly. He was just in the wrong place at the wrong time. There aren't really any such things as witches."

Lewis smiled to himself, but he said nothing. They went up to a turret, where Lewis looked out a narrow window like an arrow slot, imagining himself a sturdy British archer defending the keep. After a little while the two new friends went outside. Lewis noticed that Bertie shaded his eyes when they first came into the sunlight. "Does the light bother you?" Lewis asked.

Bertie shrugged. "I can see—just a little. I can

tell light from dark, anyway. And if there was a strong light behind you, and you moved, I could see that. But if you didn't move, you might be a chair or a shrub or almost anything. Oh, speaking of shrubs, let me show you something really interesting."

The two boys crossed the circular drive at the front of the house and went down a gentle slope. Ahead, Lewis saw the great untidy mass of hedges. They walked right up to it. The bushes were more than twice the boys' height, and their tops were raggedly overgrown. "Let's find the entrance," said Bertie.

"What entrance?" asked Lewis. How in the world did you enter a hedge?

"I'll show you," said Bertie. "Is there a tree off to our left?"

"Yes," answered Lewis.

"Good. Then move right until you find the break in the hedge. I'll be right behind you."

They edged along. Soon Lewis saw that the hedge was not a solid wall. An opening about four feet wide broke the hedge line. Overhead, the bushes had grown almost together again, so the opening was like an arch. "Here it is," said Lewis.

"Let's go in."

As soon as they stepped through the break, Lewis whistled. "It's a maze!" he said, impressed. "Oh boy! I've read about these, but I've never seen one!"

"We went in the wrong side, really," said Bertie. "The idea was that visitors would come from the road side and find their way through to the house side. But Mr Barnavelt says that it's silly to lose your guests, so he hasn't bothered with the maze for years and years. It's pretty badly grown up, but we can still find our way through it. Only don't tell my mum. She doesn't like me playing here."

"Let's go!" said Lewis. They turned left and plunged into a series of twists and turns. Before long, Lewis had no idea of where they were or which way led back out of the maze. On either side, leafy green walls hemmed them in. Originally gravel had covered the paths between the walls. Grass and weeds had sprouted through the gravel. Now the brushy growth was knee high in places, and walking through it was like wading through water. At other places, the hedges overhead had grown so far out of control that the top shoots interlaced. Sometimes it was more like walking through a green tunnel than threading through a maze. Lewis remembered that tunnels and closed-in places were one of the few things that scared his friend Rose Rita. He felt a bit braver than usual, because things like tunnels did not really get to him. Still, after a good many sharp corners and dead ends, he began to feel anxious. "Can we get out of here?" he asked Bertie.

Bertie, who clomped along behind Lewis, smiled. "Sure," he said. "Have we passed the stone bench yet?"

"About a hundred times," said Lewis.

"Let's find it again, and then I'll get us out." Bertie sounded so confident that he gave Lewis renewed determination. They wandered about in the labyrinth for a few more minutes.

"Here's the bench," said Lewis. It was a little grey stone bench, streaked black by weather and overgrown with patchy green moss. Its back was against one of the busy walls, and its seat was about wide enough for three grown-ups or four children to sit on side by side.

"Show me where it is," said Bertie, putting his hand out.

Lewis took Bertie's wrist and guided his hand to the bench. "Here," he said. "How does that help us?"

Bertie ran his hand over one of the mossy arms of the bench. "This is right in the centre of the maze," he explained. "From here I can tell which way we are going. It depends on whether the bench comes up on our left or our right. Since it's on this side, we can go the rest of the way through and out the front if we keep one hand on the hedges to our right."

"Oh," said Lewis. "Then there's a trick to it."

"It's a tricky kind of place," replied Bertie.

Lewis stuck his right hand out and brushed

against the hedge wall. They followed a twisting path, but at last they made a final turn and stepped out on to the overgrown front lawn. Just ahead of them ran the road, and off to their left was the small gatekeeper's cottage. Lewis noticed now for the first time that an actual gate had once stood at the drive. Two stone pillars remained, but tall shrubs half hid them. The friends walked down to the gateposts, and Lewis saw that the hinge plates had rusted to shapeless blobs of crusty red metal. The gates that had hung here were long gone.

"Hey," said Bertie, "I've thought of something else you ought to see. Would you like to find out more about your ancestor Martin Barnavelt and his withcraft trial?"

"Sure," said Lewis.

"There's a book in the study that tells all about it. Let's ask Mr Barnavelt if you may read it."

They made their way back to the house. Cousin Pelly was showing Jonathan a collection of butterflies that Pelly had captured years ago when he was a student at Oxford. He readily agreed to let Lewis see the book in question, but said he would have to find it for him. Meanwhile, Lewis and Bertie went outside to explore the grounds a little more. To Lewis's delight, Bertie knew the Sherlock Holmes stories very well. His mother read them to him. Lewis also discovered that since Bertie could not go to a regular school, his mother tutored him. She had once been a governess, and Lewis got the idea that she was a strict teacher. Bertie was very smart.

That evening after dinner Cousin Pelly said repeatedly how disappointed he was that Lewis and Jonathan would be leaving the next day. "I hardly get any visitors any more," said Pelly. "You can't think how lively you've made the old house feel."

"Well," said Jonathan, "perhaps we might stop by again before we return to America. We have some time at the end of our trip that isn't planned yet."

"Oh, do!" cried Cousin Pelly. "We've so much

catching up to do." And so it was more or less arranged. Just before Lewis started upstairs to bed, Pelly said, "Oh, yes. I almost forgot. Lewis, here is the book you asked for. Be careful with it, please."

As soon as Lewis got to bed, he propped himself up and examined the volume. It was a fairly large book, bound in brown leather with clasps of brass. The brass had turned green with age, and the leather was flaky and soft. A sweetish, spicy scent rose from it, a little like bay rum and a little like cinnamon and ginger. That pleased Lewis, who maintained that truly interesting volumes always smelled interesting. The title of the book had once been stamped in gold on the cover. Only a few flecks and traces of the gold remained, but Lewis could still read the sunken lettering: *A History of the Barnavelt Family and the Rebellion Against King Charles I*. He opened the book carefully and began to read the old print.

The book had been privately printed in 1721. Its author was James Barnavelt, "son of Martin."

Much of it was dull. The book included long lists of fathers and sons and uncles and cousins. Chapters covered this and that: family crests, land holdings, and where the Barnavelts went to college. One chapter, though, looked promising. Its title was "Of the Witch Finder, and the Troubles He Brought." Lewis settled in to read that one.

"Malachiah Pruitt," the chapter began, "was a most disagreeable, grasping, and self-righteous Fellow. His Styling himself a Witch Finder prov'd indeed a dark Day for the Barnavelt Family." The book went on to explain that the Puritans believed strongly in witches and witchcraft. Some of them—the chapter mentioned a Matthew Hopkins "of evil Memory"—set themselves up as witch finders. These men went from place to place and professed to expose men and women who practised evil sorcery. The local governments paid them for their "work." The victims often were hanged or burned at the stake. Malachiah Pruitt had originally been a "Yeoman Farmer" from Sussex. However, he had fought on the side of the Roundheads and "assisted at the Capture and cruel Execution of His Majesty, Charles I, for which his Friends did richly reward him."

In 1649, after the King's death, Pruitt came to Sussex as a witch finder. "He did lay Claim to Barnavelt Manor," Lewis read. "Pruitt and his Helpers mov'd into the Manor house, and they forc'd poor Martin Barnavelt and all his Kin to dwell in the meaner Out-Buildings." Pruitt supposedly refashioned a wine cellar as a "Chamber of Tortures." There accused witches were put to what the book ominously called "all the Tests of Suff'ring." Lewis read that the accused witches could save their lives in only one way: "If the poor Souls confess'd their Witchery, and nam'd Others as their fellow Witches, then the Court of this accursed Malachiah Pruitt contented itself with merely taking their Purses. If they did not confess, then Pruitt and his Helpers took their very Lives."

Lewis shivered a little. Somewhere in this very

house, nearly three hundred years ago, sour old Malachiah Pruitt had proclaimed the death sentence on men and women. Somewhere was a room that had been a "Chamber of Tortures," with a rack, and thumbscrews, and other devices of torment. It was spooky just to think about. No wonder the house had looked so terrible!

The book said that eventually Pruitt claimed that Martin Barnavelt was a witch. His son had written, "My dear Father was innocent of any such Charge. In my Opinion, the Malefactor Pruitt had heard Whispers that my Father remain'd faithful to the True Church. For this faithfulness, the Apostate Pruitt did loathe and despise Martin Barnavelt. Howsoever be it, 'tis certain that Pruitt did determine to try Martin Barnavelt on a Charge of Sorcery about the Middle of 1651."

The trial had gone badly for Martin Barnavelt, up to a point. Just when Pruitt was about to force a judgment of "guilty," the witch finder collapsed. "He had been taken with a sudden strong Fit of Illness," the book said. "The others, not being as firm in their evil Purpose as their Chief, at Length dismiss'd the Charges. So Martin Barnavelt went free, though he had not yet recover'd his House or his Holdings." Pruitt lived another two years, although the weird disease took its toll on him. "From that Day, he never again spake a Word," the book said. "He wither'd with wondrous Speed into a seeming ancient Age. He grew ill and feeble, and so died at last in 1653, his true Age about seven-and-forty."

And even then, Martin Barnavelt's troubles were not over. The Puritans held on to Barnavelt Manor until the Restoration in 1660. Then the new King, Charles II, suspected unfairly that Martin had been sympathetic to the Puritans. As a result, poor Martin did not win the title to Barnavelt Manor back for eight more years. When at length he did, the book said, "My Father was heartily disgusted with both Royalists and Roundheads, and vow'd he would never give either Side Advantage in any way."

Lewis yawned. The evening had grown late. He started to close the book. As he did so, the back endpaper suddenly flicked itself loose from the binding, and a square of yellowed paper fluttered out. Lewis blinked. He could see now that the endpaper was a false one. It was only a flyleaf that had been pasted around the edges to the real endpaper of the book. The paste had given way with age. Lewis picked up the little sheet that had fallen from its hiding place. Scribed faintly in faded black ink on the paper was a strange device made up of straight lines. It looks just like a maze, thought Lewis. Sleepily, he traced the path.

Then he sat up in bed, his eyes wide with excitement. He recognised this! He was looking at a map of the hedge maze!

But the map clearly showed a secret space that he and Bertie had overlooked.

Something waited to be discovered at the very heart of the labyrinth!

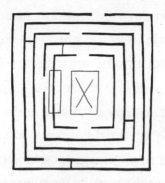

CHAPTER FOUR

Lewis lay in the dark. He could not sleep. Whenever he closed his eyes, he saw before him the drawing on the paper. He imagined himself hovering in the air above the hedge maze and looking straight down. Except that now Lewis knew something about the maze that he had not known before. Perhaps something that *no one* had known for hundreds of years. He thought about the map, which he had carefully replaced in the book. Maybe Martin Barnavelt's son had drawn it himself, leaving a chart for future members of the family to find. Something told Lewis it was a kind of treasure map. Someone had hidden something valuable away at the centre of the maze. And maybe no one had found it in nearly three hundred years! The thing to do, he told himself, is to wait until tomorrow morning and let Cousin Pelly know all about it. That would be the sensible course.

Still—what would Sherlock Holmes do? Why, he would rise, dress, take his dark lantern, and rouse Watson. "The game's afoot!" he would whisper. Then the two of them would set out on a new adventure. They would solve the mystery themselves. And at breakfast, Holmes would dramatically present Cousin Pelly with the solution to the puzzle. Lewis remembered how Holmes had made a big production out of returning the stolen papers in "The Adventure of the Naval Treaty." The detective had served the papers up at breakfast, hidden in a covered dish that was supposed to contain eggs. Lewis smiled at the memory of the happy uproar that had caused. If only he could do something like that!

Unfortunately, Lewis was timid. As he thought about venturing into the maze, he could picture all kinds of disasters that might happen. He could get lost. He could fall into a deep pit in the centre of the maze and starve to death there. He could catch pneumonia from the damp evening air. Lewis sighed. This was the curse of having a strong, active imagination. He always used it to look on the dark side. It was a part of himself that he did not like very much. Well, maybe this was an opportunity to do something about it. Slowly, he felt himself gathering all his courage. If Rose Rita were here, he thought, she would be out there in the maze right now. Rose Rita wasn't afraid of anything.

Then he remembered that Rose Rita *was* afraid of a few things. Things like tunnels, for instance. That made him feel a little braver, because he could take tunnels. For a long time Lewis lay there debating with himself. He heard a clock somewhere in the house strike twelve. The witching hour. Except that brave people like Sherlock Holmes wouldn't believe in witching hours. Lying there in the darkness, Lewis made his mind up. Just this once he would be brave. And maybe if he could be brave just this once, then the next time it would be easier. He slipped out of bed.

Before they had left for their trip, Uncle Jonathan had supervised planning and packing. Jonathan had travelled enough to know that strange bedrooms bothered him. If he had to get up in the dark, he could never get his bearings and would flounder around knocking over furniture and running into walls. Once in Detroit he had broken a hotel window because he was trying to find his way to the bathroom in the dark. To prevent similar accidents, Jonathan had bought two small, chrome-plated torches, one for himself and one for Lewis. And he had advised Lewis always to put the torch under his pillow, which was where it was right now.

Lewis took it out and turned it on for the first time. The batteries and bulb were fairly fresh, and the torch shot out a bright beam of light. It wasn't exactly a dark lantern, like the one Sherlock Holmes carried, but it was close enough. Lewis set the torch on its end, with the beam pointing up at the ceiling. That gave the room a dim illumination. It was bright enough for Lewis to slip out of bed and dress himself. Then he dug through his suitcase until he found the writing pad he planned to use to write letters to Rose Rita. He opened the book and pulled the map out. He used his mechanical pencil to copy the maze. Then he replaced the original, closed the book, and tore the copy out of his writing pad. Lewis took a very deep breath. He pulled the Sherlock Holmes deerstalker hat on to his head for added courage. He picked up his torch and tiptoed out into the hall. Now the game really was afoot!

Lewis got downstairs all right, but there the hall looked different in the beam of his torch. He took a wrong turn and had to backtrack. He tripped on a loose corner of carpeting.

Finally, though, Lewis found his way outside. The night air was cool but clear. The stars shone brightly overhead. Crickets and frogs trilled and croaked. Lewis resolutely started forward, towards the hedge maze.

He crossed the drive and felt a sudden chill of fear. He swallowed hard and hesitated. Sherlock Holmes wouldn't turn back! Well, neither would he. Lewis stepped into the unknown grass, now wet with dew, and walked on towards the maze. The legs of his corduroy trousers made *whip-whip* sounds that Lewis found surprisingly loud.

Then something swished in the grass behind him.

Lewis froze. He felt cold all over. The hair on his neck prickled. His heart thudded.

Rustle. Snap. There it was again! Something was coming after him!

Lewis shrieked and ran. Behind him footsteps began to pound. He turned to head back for the safety of the house, and found himself in a grove of trees. He was going in the wrong direction! And something was gaining on him, fast!

"Lewis! Is that you?"

"Yes!" he shouted. "Help!"

"I'm coming!" It was Bertie's voice. Bertie would save Lewis from the pursuer. He would—

Lewis suddenly realised that all the noise came from Bertie. "Oh, brother," he gasped. A second later, Bertie came blundering up, his face ghostly in the glow of the torch.

"Hello, what's up?" asked Bertie.

"You almost scared me to death," Lewis panted. His voice was shaking with fear, but he tried to make it sound angry instead: "Why did you sneak up on me like that?"

Bertie's face fell. "I'm frightfully sorry. I heard you walking about in the hallway, and I got dressed and followed you."

"You knew it was me?" asked Lewis. "How?"

Bertie sounded puzzled: "Why, from the sound of your footsteps, of course. I've been hearing them all day. What time is it, anyway? It's still quite dark, isn't it?"

"It's midnight," said Lewis. He sighed. "I was going out on a sort of mission, but now I'm not so sure."

"A mission?" asked Bertie. "Tell me about it, do!"

Lewis bit his lip. He did not want to act like a coward in front of Bertie. "Well," he said, "it started with this book. " He hastily told Bertie about the chapter in the book and the map to the maze he had found. "It looks like there is a secret place in the middle of the maze," he finished. "Or does everybody know about that already?"

"No," said Bertie slowly. "Mr Barnavelt has talked about the maze from time to time. He's always meaning to have Jenkins trim it into shape, but he never gets around to it. I'm sure that Mr Barnavelt doesn't know about any secret inside the maze, and if *he* doesn't know, then no one does." His voice became excited and eager: "I say, I think you really have discovered something! Let's go together." When Lewis did not answer at once, Bertie added,

"Come on, please let me explore with you. I could be your Dr Watson, and you could be Sherlock Holmes."

That decided Lewis. "Very well," he said, trying to make his voice sound deep and brave. "I have my, uh, dark lantern with me. The game's afoot! Come along, Watson, and we shall unravel this mystery!" Despite his misgivings, Lewis grinned. It felt great to be playing the role of the brave detective.

Bertie led the way out of the grove of trees. Since he could hardly see anyway, it made no difference to him whether it was day or night. In a few minutes the two friends stood at the entrance to the maze. They went inside. The leafy walls loomed all around them, green and impenetrable in the glow from the torch. Lewis studied the copy of the map as they made all the twists and turns. "What do you think it is?" asked Bertie after a minute or two. "The secret in the centre, I mean?"

"I don't know," said Lewis. "It looks like a kind of hidden compartment. It's almost square, and it looks hollow. If the map is right, it should be about the size of a small room. It might be anything."

"Treasure, perhaps?" asked Bertie in an excited tone.

"Sure!" said Lewis. "Why not? Maybe the Barnavelts hid their family valuables there when the Civil War broke out. We might find jewels and gold and silver. We could be rich!"

"I wish—" began Bertie. He broke off and then said, "No, never mind."

"What?" asked Lewis. They had stopped at an intersection, and he was studying the map in the torch beam. "Come on. Holmes and Watson don't keep secrets from each other."

"Well, I wish we might find enough money so that I could travel to America," whispered Bertie. "My mum is saving so that we can go there someday. The doctors here think I might— that an operation could—" He broke off and sniffled. "Oh, what's the use?"

Lewis's conscience gave him a twinge of regret. He had lain in the dark for hours trying to work up the courage to come out here. Bertie had been in the dark for years, and he had jumped at the chance to come out into the spooky maze at midnight. There was real bravery. Lewis cleared his throat. "An operation might let you see again?"

"Yes," said Bertie. "It's chancy, though."

"But you have to go to America for the operation, huh?"

"Yes," said Bertie. "You see, there are only a few surgeons in the world who would even try it. The best of them is a specialist in New York City. But it will take years and years to save up the money for the trip. And every year that I stay blind means the operation has a smaller chance of success."

Lewis took a deep breath. Oh, well, he thought, the maze isn't all *that* scary, even at night. Not if there's a friend along. He clapped Bertie on the shoulder. "Come along, Watson," he said. "Perhaps we may find the answer to our problems at the centre of the maze!"

The two friends plunged ahead, following the

twisty course of the labyrinth. Before long they stood in the narrow part of the maze before the mossy stone bench. "All right," said Lewis. "According to the map, the secret space is just behind this hedge. Now we have to find our way through!"

That proved easier said than done. The hedges grew very thick. Lewis could find no way to penetrate them. He and Bertie ranged all around the central square without success. Finally they sat on the chilly stone bench and pondered. The torch batteries were beginning to weaken, and the beam of light was now a little yellowish. "I guess the only way in is to cut through the hedges," said Lewis with a sigh. "And we'd better not do that."

"No," said Bertie, sounding disappointed. "I don't believe Mr Barnavelt would like that. You'd think that the map would show a way in."

Lewis studied the map again. This time he noticed something he hadn't before. The little rectangle that represented the stone bench looked funny, somehow. Lewis realised that the line showing the hedge passed right through it. Had the original been split that way, or had he made a mistake in copying? Lewis thought back. He was almost sure that his copy of the map was accurate. Still, what did it mean? The back of the bench was right against the hedge. It was impossible for the shrubbery to grow right through the middle of the bench.

Unless, he thought, there was another bench just like this one inside the secret opening.

Lewis jumped off the bench. "Aha!" he shouted. "Now I have it!"

Bertie rose. "What is it, Lewis?" he asked.

Lewis got on his hands and knees. Tall grass and weeds grew thickly in front of the bench. He pushed these away and shone his torch beam under the bench. He saw a dark opening. "Here," he said. "This is the way in. We have to crawl under the bench!"

Bertie groped, felt the edge of the seat, and dropped to his knees. "I'll go first," he said. He crept out of sight.

Lewis, left alone on his side of the bench, felt his heart racing. All his borrowed bravery had evaporated. The dark, narrow opening was like the jaws of death. Still, his stalwart friend had gone through—

"I say!" Bertie called. "There's a building or something in here!"

Lewis took a deep breath and drew on all his resolve. "I'm coming, Watson," he said. Then he crawled beneath the bench and into the strange clearing at the heart of the maze.

CHAPTER FIVE

"Wow!" Lewis stood in a gravelled clearing. It was not like the paths through the maze. Not a blade of grass or a spear of weed grew here. However, it was obvious that no groundskeeper took care of the weeding and mowing. The place looked as if no one had been inside it in years. The hedges were even more untidy on this side, although their branches twisted away from the central open space. Oddly, no dead leaves had collected on this side, although the gravel underfoot lay old and black from years of weathering. Behind Lewis was a stone bench, just like the one on the other side of the hedge. Except this one was clear of moss. It was as if plant life refused to nourish in this secret enclosure. The whole place was weird and spooky.

And the spookiest thing in the clearing stood right in front of Lewis.

The "building" that Bertie had mentioned was a small brick structure. It came up to Lewis's chest—about three and a half feet, he estimated. The brick was pale red and crumbling. The top of the structure was stone, with rounded edges so that rain would run off. In the very centre of the top was a dome. It was about the size of Mrs Zimmermann's largest mixing bowl, if the bowl were inverted to rest on its rim. This dome was made of stone too, like the rest of the lid. "What do you think it is?" asked Bertie, running his hand over the brick.

"I don't know," admitted Lewis. It might be anything. It could be some kind of storage building, though it was very low for that

purpose. It might be a doghouse—it might even be a dog *apartment,* with spaces for half a dozen hounds to sleep. Or it might be a tomb. Lewis shuddered, feeling goosebumps rise on his arms and legs. "Do you have a strange feeling?" he asked Bertie, his voice a squeak.

"Yes," Bertie whispered. "It's like, oh, like the whole world is holding its breath. But I think you should take a good look at this thing. It's what we came for, isn't it?"

"You're right." Lewis clenched his teeth. What good would it do to come this far and then go back without really exploring? None at all. He hoped the batteries in his torch would hold out for a while longer. "Come on. Let's find the entrance."

They walked slowly around the brick structure. It was about three feet wide by five feet long. It really was too small to be a tomb, Lewis told himself. At least, too small for an adult tomb. Bertie might fit inside—or Lewis. *Stop that*! Lewis told himself silently. Whatever the thing was, it looked solid. And as their trip around it proved, it had no entrance at all. The four walls were all unbroken by any opening, as was the stone lid.

"Nothing," said Lewis. "No doors, no grates, no way in." He had to admit that he felt relieved. His courage had been stretched very far already tonight. He did not know if it could stand much more tension without snapping altogether.

"Perhaps there's a secret door," suggested Bertie. "Let's look again."

Lewis sighed. He had no better suggestion, so the two went slowly around the brick construction once again, this time feeling for concealed levers or buttons that might release a hidden door and cause it to pivot open, the way fireplaces and bookcases were always doing in the movies. They found nothing at all. Finally, Lewis said, "Well, we can tell Cousin Pelly that this thingamajig is here, anyway. Maybe he can find a way to open it up. Or maybe he won't even mind smashing into the thing. I guess it *could* be a vault concealing the Barnavelt family treasure."

Bertie nodded in a disappointed way. "All right," he said. "But it would be ever so much more fun to find out what's inside ourselves."

"Yeah," agreed Lewis. "But my flashlight won't last too much longer, and I don't wanna be around here when it's pitch dark."

"Your flashlight? Oh—you mean your electric torch."

"Yeah," said Lewis. He had forgotten for the moment that the English had lots of different names for things. The "hood" of a car was the car's roof to an Englishman. What an American called the hood was the "bonnet" to the English. A flashlight was an electric torch here. Jonathan had told Lewis that someone had described the Americans and the English as "two cultures divided by a common language." Now Lewis said to Bertie, "Well, my, uh, *torch* is starting to burn kind of low, so maybe we'd better start back."

"I can find our way back even in the dark," Bertie said. "I don't need a light—"

"Bertie," said Lewis, in an exasperated voice.

"It's late and it's cold and my feet are wet. It's time to give up and go back home."

"All right," sighed Bertie. Lewis could tell that his friend was downcast by this turn of events. The two crunched around the edge of the brick vault—for Lewis now thought of the structure as a vault of some kind—and headed for the stone bench. The pathway between the hedge and the vault was only a couple of feet wide. It was even narrower at the bench, because the bench took up part of the room.

"I'll go first this time," Lewis said. He bent over and dropped to all fours. The sharp gravel was uncomfortable beneath his hands and knees. He had to squirm to make an abrupt turn here in order to get his head and shoulders beneath the bench. He braced one foot against the brick vault and pushed himself forward. Something gave with a hollow, grating sound.

"What was that?" asked Bertie. "Did you hear that?"

Lewis backed out and stood up again. "I heard it," he said. "I think there's a loose brick here somewhere." He directed his torch beam against the bricks. They all looked crumbly and weathered. He crouched and began to run his hands over them. "It was right in here somewhere."

Bertie hunched down beside him and began to feel the bricks too. They shoved and tugged, but all seemed solid. Then Bertie cried out, "Here's something!" He pushed again, and a brick wriggled in place, sending a little shower of red dust down. "This one is loose. "

"Yeah," agreed Lewis. He pushed the brick too. The mortar around the edges had disintegrated over the years. Friction alone held the brick in its place. "You work that end of it," directed Lewis, "and I'll see what I can do with this one."

The two rocked the brick back and forth in a sort of seesaw motion. At first it would barely move. Then it loosened and began to slip back. A little patter of brick dust and particles showered down on to the gravel. Now when Bertie pushed his end, Lewis's swung out about a quarter of an inch. Lewis tried to grasp the brick between his thumb and fingers, but the edges were rounded and worn smooth, and he could not get a good grip. "Rock it some more," he said to Bertie.

They must have spent five or six minutes at the task.

Gradually Lewis became aware that the moon was up, bright enough to give them some light. He switched off the torch to save the batteries. They ground away at the brick some more. The brick slipped back in its place. When they paused, it was definitely sunken, its face an inch or more farther into the wall than those of the surrounding bricks. "A little more," said Bertie, exploring with his fingers the edge of the opening they were making. "If it won't come out this way, maybe we can push it through."

Scrape. Grind. By fractions of inches, the brick moved. Lewis's fingers began to ache from the pressure. He was sweating and getting grumpy. After all, he thought, what will this get us? We sure can't squeeze through this hole, and we might not even be able to look through it to see what's inside—

Plop! The brick dropped through. Lewis caught his breath. He reached for his torch. It rolled away on the gravel, and he fumbled to pick it up. He began, "Let's have a look—"

Whoosh! Hot air blasted into his face from the hole the brick had left. Lewis gagged. The air stank of rot and decay. Bertie cried out.

And something laughed, something big and horrible. Lewis screamed. He found the torch, but now he had no interest in peering into the vault. "Run!" he yelled to Bertie.

Bertie was already worming his way through the opening beneath the stone bench. As soon as his legs disappeared, Lewis followed. The horrible laugh sounded again. It was deep, sinister, and angry. It bubbled in an awful way, as if it were coming from a huge, decaying chest. Something with claws closed on Lewis's ankle, and he yanked his foot away. He heard a terrifying growl as he popped through the opening and into the maze. Then he began to run. His Sherlock Holmes hat nearly fell off. He clapped one hand on top to hold it on, and with the other he tried to find the switch for his torch. He ran into a hedge, all prickly twigs and branches. And it grabbed him.

Lewis felt the thin branches curling down to hold his arms and legs. He screamed and flailed away. The branches snapped and tore. He finally got the torch on, and the first thing he saw was bright-red blood oozing from the broken twigs.

At first Lewis had the panicky thought that he had been wounded—then he saw that the blood was coming from the broken branches! The bleeding hedge writhed away from the light. With a shriek, Lewis beat at the pieces of twig that had curled around his arms. They were creeping over his jacket, humping and lifting their blunt ends like horrible worms. He flicked them off and staggered away. Something snuffled behind him, sounding like a gigantic hound hot on his trail. He ran desperately down the dark alley of one of the hedge paths.

"I see thee!" Lewis heard the voice inside his head. It was a soft voice, mocking and ancient and evil. He did not dare look back. He took another turn, and then another.

He was completely lost in the maze now. "Aye, run!" purred the voice. "It makes the chase so much more interesting." Somehow Lewis could tell that the voice came from overhead.

He looked up, dreading what he would see. At first there was nothing: just the starry sky and the moon beaming down through the narrow space at the top of the hedges. Then Lewis realised that the moon was *wrong*. He had seen the Man in the Moon before, the illusory face caused by the seas and the craters on the full moon. This was different. The pale, waning moon had an odd shape, and the markings on it were growing darker—

"Now I have thee!" The moon had become a leering skull. The eye sockets were dark and endless, and two hateful red sparks glowed deep in them, staring down at Lewis. The skull was missing teeth both top and bottom, and the

gap-toothed mouth swung open in an awful, soundless laugh. "Now I have thee!" the voice said again, and this time the skull's mouth moved in rhythm with the words.

Lewis screamed, but all that came out was a high-pitched, thin screech. He closed his eyes and blundered on. Again he heard growls, and then a snuffling sound behind him, and the hedges began to rustle. It was as if a monstrous animal, a lion or a tiger, were squeezing its way through the hedge walls, running him down. It was a trick, some part of Lewis's mind shouted at him. The hideous skull-moon was a trick, making him freeze and hesitate until the—the *thing* behind him could catch up.

He desperately turned a corner. And found himself trapped. He had run into a dead end.

Lewis whirled. He shone his torch down the maze path. The leaves and twigs moved at the very edge of the beam. He heard a coughing roar. Twin spots of green suddenly glowed at him, like the eyes of a beast. But the growling, stalking creature itself was invisible. Lewis thought he would faint. He tried to scream again and could only hiss—

"This way!" Something grabbed his arm! He felt himself being tugged into the hedge wall! Lewis struggled to escape. "It's me!" the voice cried. "It's Bertie!"

The invisible creature roared again. Lewis scrambled through the scratching hedges. "You're almost free," Bertie panted. "Come on!"

With a final effort Lewis jerked his leg loose. They were on the grass outside the hedge maze, not far from the side entrance of the house. "Run for the Manor!" shouted Bertie.

Lewis realised that they had not escaped yet. Something was clawing at the hedges and soon would be through. He heard hoarse rasps of breath, low growls. Following Bertie, Lewis turned and ran as fast as he could up the hillside. He dashed across the asphalt driveway—

And tripped.

Lewis went sprawling in the wet grass. He lost his grip on the torch. It hit the ground, flared brightly, and went out.

Behind him something dark bounded through the moonlight. It had no definite body, just a shapeless form, a shadow a little darker than the night. Lewis tried to get up, but he had twisted his ankle and it would not hold his weight. Where was Bertie? The horrible thing reached the opposite edge of the drive—

It stopped dead.

Lewis scrambled away on all fours, like a demented crab. Then Bertie was beside him again, pulling at his arm. His twisted ankle sent a flare of pain up his leg, but Lewis staggered to his feet. He looked back, sobbing.

The hillside lay perfectly quiet in the moonlight.

"It—it's gone," whimpered Bertie. "Whatever it was."

A soft breeze made the grass and trees rustle. Then a lone cricket began to chirp. Another one joined in, and then a third. Lewis realised that every living thing around the Manor had fallen silent when that horror had come from the vault. Now the world was beginning to breathe again. His torch lay in the grass, the metal gleaming in the moonlight. Lewis stooped and picked it up. "I wo-wonder if we're sa-safe now," he gasped. He wiped his eyes on the sleeve of his jacket.

"D-do you think we should tell anyone?" asked Bertie, sounding as frightened as Lewis.

Lewis suddenly got the shakes. He trembled violently, and he felt as if he were going to burst out screaming. "No," he said. He sniffled and tried to control himself. "M-maybe it's really gone for good. I th-think we'd better keep this to ourselves."

"Whatever you say." Bertie sounded relieved. Lewis guessed that his friend dreaded what his mother might say about their nocturnal adventure. Lewis knew that he did not want to confess anything to Uncle Jonathan.

They went inside, and Bertie went along with Lewis as far as his bedroom door. Lewis slipped inside, undressed, and climbed into bed. He lay there shivering and weeping. He thought back to the prayers he knew, but they brought him little comfort. Lewis understood that something ghastly had come out of that mysterious vault. And he sensed that some terrible and insatiable force was now loose upon the world. He had no idea of when—or how—it would all end.

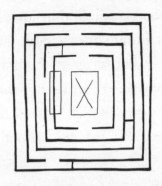

CHAPTER SIX

Jonathan knocked on Lewis's door at seven-thirty. "Time for breakfast," he called. "Up and at 'em!"

The noise woke Lewis up. He hadn't got much sleep after the wild chase. He felt groggy and exhausted and miserable, but he climbed out of bed. It was a grey, cloudy morning. Everything outside appeared drained of life. In other words, it looked very much like an ordinary English day. Lewis sighed and got ready for breakfast.

He found his cousin and his uncle downstairs in the small dining room. Mrs Goodring had brought in a big platter of scrambled eggs, which Pelly boasted came from their very own hens. On another platter were a few pieces of British bacon, which Lewis thought was more like ham.

There was also orange marmalade, fresh butter, a basket of warm toast, a large pot of coffee, and a small pitcher of hot cocoa. He nibbled on some toast and tried a few forkfuls of egg. He could barely swallow them, because he felt a little dizzy from lack of sleep and his stomach was queasy. Jonathan glanced at him with some concern. "What's wrong, Lewis?" he asked. "Not getting sick, are you?"

Lewis shook his head. "Just tired," he mumbled. "I didn't sleep very well last night. I guess I'm still not used to travelling."

Pelly smiled, but the smile was forced and strained. "Difficult sleeping in a strange place, what? Nothing to be ashamed of, my boy. Must be a family ailment. I've often noticed myself how hard it— What was that?" He sprang up from his chair and froze in a kind of crouch. His grey eyes grew round in alarm, and his gaze darted towards the window. Lewis gasped and spun to look over his shoulder.

But he could see nothing unusual through the window. Nothing except the overgrown hedge maze halfway down the front lawn. He heard his elderly cousin sigh, and he looked back across the table. Pelly sank very gradually back into his chair, like a balloon slowly deflating. His face was pale, and beads of sweat had broken out on his forehead. His silvery hair all stood on end in wild disarray, as if he had seen something truly hair-raising. He fished a large, frayed handkerchief from his side pocket and mopped his face. "Sorry," he said with a sickly smile. "I could have sworn I saw someone sneaking about out there. Nerves, I suppose. I really should have guests more often.

Simply out of practice as a host, I fear. The excitement of your visit has probably put me on edge—not that I mean to say you are unwelcome, you understand."

"Of course," said Jonathan smoothly. "Do you ever get any trespassers here, cousin?"

Pelly fluttered his fingers in a dismissive gesture. "Oh, the odd person now and again. Mrs Goodring feeds them and they go on their way. Barnavelt Manor is a very isolated estate, you know. If a disaster occurred and wiped us all out, I expect it would be weeks before someone in the village even noticed. Ha-ha." His laugh sounded faint and artificial, and neither Jonathan nor Lewis joined in. "Well, that was a bad joke, I must say," Pelly added in a lame voice.

Lewis finished his cocoa and looked out the window again. The grey sky hung low and oppressive over the landscape. The light filtering through the flat cloud layer was weird and unusual. In it, the summer greens had taken on a lurid hue. The grass and trees looked yellow and ill in the muted gloom. And everything lay still and breathless, with not a blade of grass stirring. Lewis remembered a summer day like this back home. He and Jonathan had gone with Mrs Zimmermann and Rose Rita out to Mrs Zimmermanns cottage on Lyon Lake for swimming and a picnic. They did not get to do either, because a black, threatening cloud had suddenly erupted in the sky. Within a matter of minutes, everything had grown dark and hushed. "Uh-oh," Mrs Zimmermann had said. "The calm before the storm." And what a storm had broken out only a few minutes later! Lewis remembered how frightened he had been at the crackling, jagged forks of brilliant lightning, the explosions of thunder, and the howling of the wind. Lightning ripped the bark right off a tall pine tree down beside the lake. Later they learned that a tornado had whipped through the woods not three miles from the lake cottage.

And this calm was a lot like that one, Lewis thought uneasily. Everything too quiet, too still. Except—

He blinked and felt a chill. Was he dreaming? No, it was as he thought. Everything was as lifeless as a statue. Except the hedge maze. It was moving! The bushes stirred, and their thin branches waved and curled. It couldn't be the wind, because the trees near the maze were perfectly still, their leaves hanging limp and motionless. And now that he noticed, the hedge twigs were clenching and unclenching. They did not look like branches touched by wind, but like long, leafy fingers clutching up at the sky. Lewis shuddered. Then he turned and looked wildly at Jonathan.

Jonathan saw Lewis's frightened expression and raised his eyebrows. "What in heaven's name is the matter, Lewis?" he asked. "You look like you've seen a ghost with hairy feet and a ten-gallon hat!"

Cousin Pelly frowned at him. Lewis looked back at the hedge maze. He blinked. The hedges were quiet again, just as unmoving as everything else. They might as well have been part of a landscape painting. Had he imagined it all? Lewis realised that Jonathan was waiting for some kind of answer. He swallowed his fear.

"Uh—nothing, Uncle Jonathan," muttered Lewis. "It just looks kind of stormy outside, that's all. Uh, may I be excused? I'd like to say goodbye to Bertie before we have to leave."

"Of course," said Pelly. "By all means. And we'll have to see if we can plan something exciting for you two to do when you come back in August, what? Run along, Lewis." Lewis slipped out of his chair and left the room. Just as he got outside the door, he overheard Pelly murmuring to Jonathan: "One can't blame the lad for being out of sorts this morning. I feel it too—don't you? Some kind of dashed odd gloom in the air. As if something terrible is waiting to happen."

Jonathan spoke a reply too softly for Lewis to hear. He gulped. The air felt thick and heavy, as if something had sucked all the oxygen out of it. You're being silly, Lewis told himself. He went in search of Bertie. His friend was in his own ground-floor bedroom, dressed but lying sprawled on the bed and listening to the radio. "Hello, Lewis," he said as soon as he heard the other boy's footsteps. "I had a rotten night. How about you?"

"Same here," admitted Lewis. "And today everyone is feeling upset. " He sat in a high-backed Victorian chair and looked out the window. He was grateful that the windows in Bertie's room had a view of the back lawn, the distant, empty barn, the hen run, and the vegetable garden. Lewis had seen enough of the front lawn and the terrible hedge maze. "We'll be leaving in an hour or so, I guess," said Lewis. "I hope it's all over."

"What?" asked Bertie.

Lewis shrugged, and then realised that Bertie could not see him shrug. "I don't know," he said. "Whatever it was we started last night. I wish we'd never gone into that stupid maze. I wish I'd never read about old Martin Barnavelt and his stupid trial for witchcraft."

"Well," said Bertie reasonably, "we did, and you did. What's done can't be undone. The question is, what is left to do? What do you think?"

Lewis grimaced. He hated having the weight of that decision on his shoulders. He felt helpless and small and weak. He hadn't *meant* to bring anything evil down on the household! Now Bertie was asking him what they should do. How was he supposed to know? He thought for a minute. What would Sherlock Holmes do? Of course, Holmes had never had a case quite like this, involving a real ghost—or at least something *like* a real ghost. True, there was the matter of the Hound of the Baskervilles. Everyone had thought the Hound was some kind of spirit. Maybe what Holmes did in that story was the answer. Lewis cleared his throat. "Uh, Bertie, remember how Sherlock Holmes sent Dr Watson to Baskerville Hall?"

Bertie smiled. "Sure. That's one of my favourites!"

"Well," said Lewis, "that's what I want to do in this case. You are my Dr Watson. Your job is to occupy Barnavelt Manor here and keep track of everything. I'll write out our itinerary for you. You can get your mum to send me a postcard in care of whatever hotel we're staying in to alert me if anything goes wrong."

Bertie shook his head. "I don't know. Wouldn't that mean I'd have to tell her about—about what you and I did last night? And the hedge maze, and the horrible sounds? I really don't want to, you know." He sounded frightened.

Lewis got up and began to pace the floor. "Well, why don't we think up a code? Just work some phrase into the message that would tell me how everything is going. You could say, 'The weather has been wonderful here,' if things are all right. If anything bad should happen, you could say, 'We had a storm recently.' How is that?"

"No, that wouldn't work," said Bertie in a reasonable voice. "Because what if we had a week of rain and I wanted to report that things were all right? Or what if it was sunny and old Growly came out of the maze? I couldn't say the day was stormy, then. My mum would think I'd gone right off my chump if I didn't even know what the weather was like."

"Right," said Lewis, mentally kicking himself for overlooking the obvious. "I hadn't thought about that. OK, what about this? Our code words for everything's being ordinary will be 'wonderful' and 'fine' and 'good.' If you work one of those into a message, then I'll know Barnavelt Manor is normal and everyone is all right. But if something goes wrong, then write a message with 'frightfully' or 'awfully' or 'terribly' in it. Then I'll know you need help, and somehow I'll get Uncle Jonathan to come straight back to Barnavelt Manor."

Bertie agreed that this was a good idea. He repeated the code words a couple of times to make sure he would remember them. Lewis got a pad and pencil and wrote out a list of hotels and cities where he and Jonathan would be staying. Lewis promised to keep in touch by dropping Bertie a card at least once a week. Soon after that, Jonathan hunted Lewis up. Cousin Pelly had fired up the engine of the cantankerous Austin Seven, and it was time to leave.

The car trip out to the railway station was subdued. On the platform, Pelly shook hands with Jonathan and Lewis. "Well," he said, "you two have a ripping holiday, and then hurry back to stay with us for a week or so. Can't tell you how much I've enjoyed meeting you both. There are still lots of stories yet to tell." His words sounded hearty, but his smile flickered uncertainly on his anxious face, like a candle flame fighting a cold breeze. Jonathan and Lewis boarded their train. Lewis looked out the window. The last thing he saw was Cousin Pelly standing tall and dejected on the platform, his hands in his pockets, his shoulders stooped. He looked like a frail and sad old stork.

CHAPTER SEVEN

In the days that followed, Lewis shook off some of the melancholy that had descended on him. He and Jonathan took a ferry across the English Channel, and then a train to Paris. There they saw all the sights: the Louvre Museum, the Champs-Élysées, and the Eiffel Tower, among other things. They ate at pavement cafes and stopped on the Left Bank of the Seine to watch art students dabbing away at landscapes. They shopped in more out-of-the-way little stores, and Jonathan showed off his French, which was barely adequate to order a meal or to ask, "How much is this, please?"

However, even with all the touristy distractions, Lewis did not neglect his promise to keep in touch with Bertie. On the morning of their arrival in Paris, Lewis immediately sent a picture postcard off to him. Then on the last day of their stay in the French capital, Lewis received a card from Bertie. Bertie's mother had beautifully clear, old-fashioned handwriting. The message was:

Dear Lewis,
Thanks ever so much for the wonderful card. I hope your and your uncle's holiday is lots of fun, and I'll be glad to see you back here again in August.
Your friend, Bertie

Lewis sighed in relief and began to feel a little better. The very first thing he had noticed in the message was the code word "wonderful." At least their system was working and everything was calm and normal back at Barnavelt Manor—so far.

Jonathan and Lewis continued their journey. They left Paris for Marseilles, a French seaport on the Mediterranean Sea, and from there they travelled to Rome with its Vatican City. Then they continued down the coast of Italy to Naples, where the great volcano Vesuvius sent plumes of vapour into the blue Italian sky. Lewis was fascinated by Pompeii, which had once been a Roman city. The volcano had erupted violently in AD 79, and a rain of volcanic ash had buried Pompeii, petrifying everything just as it had been on that last terrible day. It was spooky to walk the dead streets and think about the crowds of panic-stricken Romans fleeing from the wrath of Vesuvius. It made Lewis very jumpy. What if the mountain should blow its top again? Then in two thousand years people might come to see Lewis and his uncle, turned to stone in the streets of Pompeii. A fossilised Jonathan would still be holding his stone Kodak up tó take a

picture, and a fossilised Lewis would pose smiling in front of an ancient Roman temple. Just thinking about it gave Lewis the creeps.

But the volcano slumbered on, and the two travellers continued their holiday. At every stop Lewis sent a flurry of brightly coloured picture postcards. Most of them went back to New Zebedee, to Rose Rita and Mrs Zimmermann. Lewis shopped conscientiously for these, trying to find cards that were appropriate. For Rose Rita he chose cards with pictures of castles and cannon and armour, and for Mrs Zimmermann he looked for cards showing lots of purple flowers. But any postcard would do for Bertie, although Lewis tried to find pictures that Mrs Goodring could easily describe to him. Lewis sent cards to Bertie practically every other day. Meanwhile, two more cards came from Bertie, each one containing a code word to signify that life continued untroubled at the Manor.

As the trip went on, Lewis not only began to feel a little easier in his mind; he also began to feel better physically. Every day he and Jonathan walked for miles to see the sights. In many of the countries they visited, the food proved strange and unpalatable—at least to Lewis's taste. He did not understand how the French could relish snails, or the Germans blood-red sausages oozing oil on to a bed of pungent sauerkraut. Even when the food was delicious, like the wonderful Italian pasta, Lewis had surprisingly little appetite. All the fascinating new sights distracted him, so for once everything around him was more interesting than food.

As a result, Lewis did not eat nearly as heartily as he always had back home. It was in Italy, while they were touring Venice, that he first noticed the resulting change. He was getting dressed one morning when for some reason his belt felt funny. He looked down. Ordinarily he fastened the belt in the very first hole. The leather had a groove worn in it where the buckle clamped it down. This morning the belt was too loose when he fastened it in that hole. Lewis tightened it. The belt fastened in the next hole snugly but comfortably. His waist had shrunk by about an inch.

Lewis blinked. He remembered the insulting names the boys at school were always calling him: Blimp, Tubby, and Lard Ass. A long time ago one of the boys, Tarby, had called him a fatso and had sneered, "Why don't ya lose some weight?" And Lewis had tried, but without any success. Once he had even sent off for a Charles Atlas bodybuilding book, but the exercises were boring and he kept at them for only a few days. He had just about resigned himself to being fat all his life. Now without even consciously trying, he had lost some weight. And when he thought about it, he never felt really hungry. Lewis grinned. Oh, boy, he thought. If I can just keep this up, won't Rose Rita and Mrs Zimmermann be surprised!

Fortunately, the routine proved easy to continue. At every stop Jonathan insisted on walking from site to site, climbing miles of stairs in museums and cathedrals and monuments, and sampling the local cuisine. As their trip took them from Venice to Vienna and then up into Germany, Lewis tightened his belt a second notch. He seemed to have more stamina too, and his legs stopped aching as he became accustomed to all the walking. Lewis noticed that Jonathan was also losing weight. His uncle had a potbelly that swelled his red vest out, but all the walking they did began to make that shrink. Maybe the holiday would be good for both of them, Lewis thought.

However, Lewis had to admit that one thing threatened to spoil all the fun he was having. It did not happen often: maybe once a week. It was a terrible dream. In the dream, Lewis was lost in an overgrown field. A few leafless trees grew here and there, and everywhere else the dead yellow grass stood knee high. Strange bushes poked up through the grass. The bushes had red, writhing, wormlike branches and twigs, and the leaves on them were the same crimson colour as blood. In the dream it was always the same kind of day: overcast and dark. And Lewis always had the uneasy notion that he had to get somewhere very fast. But he did not know where he was supposed to go or what he had to do when he arrived. Worse, with the sky so gloomy and the sun hidden from view, he could not even judge directions.

So he stayed in the centre of the field while a feeling of dread grew stronger and stronger. Finally he could stand it no more, and he began to walk. The tough yellow grass snared his ankles and threatened to trip him. The bushes began to stir and rustle, though Lewis could feel no breeze. Then he could see that the bushes were straining to reach out and grab him. They wanted to wrap those horrible red tentacle-like branches around his arms and legs.

In the dream Lewis started to run. He could hardly drag his feet. It was like running through treacle, or like trying to run with concrete blocks strapped to both feet. And he heard a horrible sound of thick breathing, as if some monstrous giant lay hidden just out of his sight. The humid air smelled mouldy and rank, the smell of decaying plants and slimy earthworms and damp dirt. Somehow, one of the awful bushes suddenly sprang up right in front of him. He tried to stop, but the waving grass felt like the ocean pounding against his legs. It swept him forward, inch by inch. And as it pushed him closer, he saw something dreadful. At the base of the bush sat a human skeleton. The red shoots of the bush grew through its ribs, caressing them, clamping them, and holding the skeleton in position. The skull lolled down on the ribs. As the grass shoved Lewis forward, the skull slowly rose. The bush was growing as Lewis watched, like plants he had seen in an animated film. The fleshless skull tipped back and back until he could see the face.

Green-glass spectacles covered the eye sockets. "Bertie!" screamed Lewis. Only his voice came out as a whisper that ripped his throat.

The skull's jaw dropped open. It appeared to laugh silently at him. And then the glasses moved. Red twigs grew out of the eye sockets, waving and squirming like handfuls of worms.

The horrible, writhing shoots pushed the glasses off. The spectacles dropped to the ground.

And now Lewis was so close that the branches began to wrap around his arms, drawing him closer to the hungry bush. The leaves had saw-toothed edges, and Lewis felt a million of them begin to cut into his face and hands and arms—

And then he would wake up, shivering and covered with clammy sweat. On the nights when he had the fearful dream, Lewis would lie awake afterwards, silently reciting all the prayers he could remember. The next night he would be afraid to go to bed, and he would lie awake for a long time, fearful of what sleep might bring. Luckily, he never had the dream two nights in a row. Still, it would return to haunt him again a week or so later.

The last time he had the nightmare was the final night that he and Jonathan were staying in Gottingen. After the nightmare had jerked him awake, Lewis did not sleep again at all that night. He got up the next morning shaky and wretched from the strain. He fumbled with his clothing so much that Jonathan asked, "Are you feeling sick or something?" in a worried tone.

Lewis shook his head. "I guess I've been too excited to sleep well," he mumbled.

Jonathan said he could understand that, but he kept looking at Lewis with evident concern. As they came down to breakfast in the hotel restaurant, Lewis and Jonathan passed the front desk. The clerk at the desk brightened when he saw them. "Some mail for the young man," he said in heavily accented English. He gave Lewis a postcard.

Lewis recognised Mrs Goodring's handwriting at once. The card bore an airmail stamp and was postmarked the day before yesterday. The message written on the front made Lewis's heart thump painfully. It was just one sentence:

Dear Lewis,
I'm awfully glad you are coming back to Barnavelt Manor soon.
Your friend, Bertie

"Awfully" was one of the code words. Something was wrong at Barnavelt Manor. And today Jonathan and Lewis would leave Germany to return to England.

Lewis had the panicky feeling that all his nightmares were about to come true.

CHAPTER EIGHT

Once again the train pulled into the country
station. Once again Jonathan and Lewis stood
on the platform surrounded by their luggage.
And once again the boxy old Austin Seven came
puttering towards them, with the tall, lean
figure of Cousin Pelly behind the wheel. But
this time Lewis felt a suffocating dread. Part
of it was the weather. The sky did not seem to
have changed since they had left Barnavelt
Manor more than a month earlier. The gloomy
grey clouds seemed so low that you could climb

up a tall ladder and touch them. The air was muggy and close, just like the oppressive atmosphere in Lewis's nightmare. The whole world seemed waiting for something to happen. Something awful and deadly.

The car creaked to a halt, and Cousin Pelly climbed out.

He clapped his bony hands together. "So home are the travellers, eh? So jolly! Ripping times await us, I can tell you!" He grinned wolfishly.

Lewis caught his breath. Was *this* his gentle, eccentric Cousin Pelly? The old man's eyes were red rimmed, and the flesh under his cheeks had sunken in. His wild silver hair had not been trimmed. His smile looked sly and knowing. Lewis felt his uncle start in surprise. Then Jonathan said, "Yes, Cousin Pelly, we have returned. It will be good to rest in the ancestral mansion tonight. I hope we aren't inconveniencing you."

Pelly gave him a sharp, suspicious look. "Inconveniencing me? Nonsense! I want to show you all the, ah, hospitality that Barnavelt

Manor affords. We have to stick together, what? After all, we are the last living male Barnavelts!" And then Pelly snickered in a most unpleasant way. "Come along, let's get your baggage loaded. I can hardly wait to get you back to the Manor!"

Jonathan and Lewis loaded the luggage into the car. Jonathan kept glancing at his oddball English cousin. He could not put his finger on it, but he knew that the old man had changed somehow, and not for the better. Jonathan sighed. He knew that something was bothering Lewis too, something that his nephew was not ready to talk about. Although Jonathan had tried hard to remain cheerful and upbeat during the long trip, he was well aware that Lewis occasionally had nightmares. Several times Lewis's groans and moans had wakened Jonathan at night. But Lewis had never complained or asked to talk about whatever was bothering him, and Jonathan felt that he should respect his nephew's privacy. He knew that sometimes people had troubles they simply had to work out for themselves.

Now, though, Jonathan began to regret not offering his help to Lewis. He waited until Lewis had squeezed into the back seat of the car, and then he climbed into the passenger seat beside Pelly. As Pelly started the ancient car, Jonathan took out his pipe. He had almost stopped smoking over the past year, and he was determined to cut out tobacco altogether as soon as his supply ran out this time. But right now he felt like a meditative pipe. He puffed away as the car careened along the narrow road towards Barnavelt Manor.

For his part, Lewis felt his discomfort increasing as they clattered between the fields of grazing sheep. He looked away from the hedge maze as Pelly turned in at the drive. That was why Lewis was looking straight at the gatekeeper's cottage as they passed it on the right. And there was a white, hollow-eyed face staring out at him. It was only a momentary glimpse, but Lewis could see the deep-set glaring eyes, the tight-lipped grin, and the clenched, crooked teeth. Lewis glanced at Jonathan, but his uncle had noticed nothing. He merely sat staring straight ahead, his pipe clenched in his teeth.

The car creaked to a weary halt in front of the Manor, and old Jenkins came out to help with the luggage again. This time the servant did not speak at all. He just gave both Jonathan and Lewis a long, disapproving gaze, as if he blamed them for the stifling weather and the general atmosphere of gloom. They took the same rooms they had occupied before, and Lewis was grateful when he reflected that a door led from his bedroom directly into Jonathan's. If he felt really frightened, he could always get up and leave the communicating door open. And maybe lock the hall door to keep the ghosts and ghouls out.

This time no mid-morning snack awaited them. Mrs Goodring told them that she would make sandwiches for lunch, but her voice was low and troubled. She kept her hands clutched in her apron as she spoke, and she kept stealing nervous glances at Cousin Pelly. If the very idea had not been absurd, Lewis would have guessed that she was afraid of the harmless old man. Lewis set off to find Bertie, who was playing, Mrs Goodring said distractedly, "somewhere about."

He found Bertie outside, behind the house. Bertie sat with his back against an oak tree, his elbows on his knees and his chin in his hands. He tilted his head as Lewis approached and said, "Who's there?"

"It's me," said Lewis ungrammatically. "We got here as soon as we could." He took a long and careful look around. Jenkins was doing something in the garden, off to the left. He was much too far away to hear the boys. No one else was around. Still, Lewis lowered his voice as he sat next to Bertie. "What's up? I got the note you sent."

Bertie took a long, deep breath. "Crikey, but I'm glad you're back. Oh, Lewis, I've had a terrible summer. Do you have bad dreams about—about you-know-what?"

Lewis flinched. He had expected trouble of some sort, but not that. "Yeah," he admitted. He hesitated, but then he went on to describe the awful nightmares to Bertie. He found that he could finally talk freely about them, since Bertie had shared his adventure in the hedge maze. It was a relief to spill out all his fears at last, even though talking about them made Lewis breathe faster and made his heart race. "So then I always wake up," he finished. "I guess you've been sleeping pretty badly too."

"Yes," Bertie said. "Only mine are sort of different. In my dream, I hear hushed sounds everywhere—from my closet, from under my bed, from outside. It's like a lot of tiny voices, speaking in whispers just too low for me to hear. Except I hear my name every once in a while— 'Mumum mumum mumum, Bertie,' the voices will say." Bertie shivered and hugged his knees against his chest. "And there are other sounds too. Sounds like an enormous spider, as big as a plate, walking slowly across the floor towards my bed. Tapping sounds at my window, like a skeleton drumming its fingers on the glass. I just lie there terrified until I wake up and the sounds stop. And sometimes I think they go on a little while after I wake up."

"Wow," Lewis said in an unsteady voice. He had never been particularly afraid of the dark, but then he could chase it away with a torch or a match. He had never considered what awful nightmares a blind person might have. "I don't think I could stand a dream like that," he admitted.

"That isn't the worst," whispered Bertie. "Two other things happened, just last week. That's why I sent you the card."

"What?" asked Lewis, though he dreaded hearing the answer.

Bertie lowered his voice even more, so Lewis had to lean close to hear him. "First, a gentleman from London came and asked to rent the gatekeeper's house. Mr Barnavelt agreed, and he moved in. But, Lewis, he's *horrible*!"

Lewis began to shiver. Get hold of yourself, he thought. You can't show Bertie that you're afraid. He cleared his throat and said, "How do you mean, 'horrible'?"

Bertie shook his head miserably. "Oh, I don't know. It's hard to describe. I was out front when Jenkins hauled his trunk into the gatekeeper's cottage, and I think the man walked past me. I felt something cold, the way you feel sometimes on a hot day if a cloud covers the sun. It was just like a cool shadow passing over me. And the man said, 'What a likely-looking lad.' Just that, and nothing more. But his voice, Lewis, sounded like those terrible whispery voices I've been dreaming about. It sounded like the voice of a ghost. And—and—I don't think I can talk about this—"

Lewis put his hand on his friend's shoulder. "You can tell me," he said. "You're good old Watson, remember?"

Bertie smiled, but Lewis saw a tear creep down from behind his green spectacles. It surprised him a little. He had not stopped to think that a blind person might be able to cry. Bertie took off his spectacles and wiped his eyes on his sleeve. Lewis noticed that he had blue eyes, and they looked normal, except the pupils were very wide and black. Bertie slipped the glasses back on and said, "Thank you, Holmes." Then he took a couple of deep breaths. "It's hard to say this, and it sounds crazy. But Lewis, the man has no footstep!"

Lewis frowned. "What do you mean?"

"You know how I got to recognise your footstep so fast?"

Lewis nodded without thinking, then said, "Yeah. That's a neat trick."

"Well, I *can't* hear this man's footsteps at all. He passed right by me, and I couldn't hear the grass rustling. He stepped up on to the threshold, and his boots made no sound at all. And twice when I've been out front, he's suddenly spoken to me from quite close by, and yet I've never heard him approach."

Lewis understood his friend's fear. Now that he thought about it, being blind and *not* hearing someone coming might be even more frightening than hearing someone you are afraid of step closer and closer. "Wh-what did he say to you?" stammered Lewis.

"Nothing important. Once he said, 'A quiet, lonely life here, eh, lad?' And the other time, he just said, 'Old houses have their own spirit, don't they?' You see, it wasn't really what he said that bothered me. It was sort of what he *didn't* say."

"Hmm," said Lewis." You mean, he might have meant 'You are all alone here, and there's no help for miles' the first time, and 'Barnavelt Manor is a haunted house' the second one. Or something like that."

"Exactly," agreed Bertie. "He was—now what is the word?—implying more than he actually said. And he knew that I would understand that."

Lewis swallowed. "What was the second bad thing that happened?"

"Promise you won't laugh?"

"Of course not," said Lewis with some surprise.

"Well—the chickens died. All of them."

"What?" Lewis did not know what to make of this news. "Did an animal kill them, or—?"

"No," Bertie said. "The morning after that strange man first showed up, Jenkins went to collect the eggs, as usual. He came back very upset. Every chicken was lying dead on the ground, but none of them had any injury. At first we thought it might be a disease, but the vet checked some of them and said he couldn't explain it. They just—died. As if something might have frightened them to death."

Lewis shuddered. He did not like this piece of news. It reminded him too much of the awful night when something had chased him and Bertie. He himself had felt almost on the verge of dying from fright then.

After a moment, Bertie went on: "And ever since Mr Prester—that's his name, Jenkins says, Mr Matthew Prester of London—moved into the cottage, Jenkins and Mr Barnavelt and even Mum have changed. They seem frightfully nervous and edgy. Mr Barnavelt snaps at me if I make any noise at all, and he's never done that. And Mum gets cross at me as easy as anything. Oh, Lewis, what are we to do?"

Lewis bit his lip. That was the million dollar question, all right: what were two boys to do when they were up against something they could not begin to comprehend? But even Sherlock Holmes must have been a boy once, Lewis reminded himself. Every great hero has to begin someplace. After a few moments, Lewis said, "OK, here's what I think. First, we can't go to Cousin Pelly and complain about this Matthew what's-his-name. I know Pelly needs the rent money, and without any evidence, he wouldn't kick this guy out of the cottage. So before we go to anybody, we have to make sure that the fellow is up to no good. I think I might have seen him when we drove in. Somebody peeked out at us from inside the cottage. He looks about as bad to me as he sounds to you. Still, you just can't go by appearances, I guess. We have to find evidence."

"Evidence of what?" asked Bertie.

"I don't know," confessed Lewis. "Something that might prove to the others that this man isn't what he seems. I'll try to question Jenkins without making him suspicious. And maybe the two of us can sneak up to the cottage and see what he is doing in there. Are you with me?"

Bertie gave him a sickly grin. "As always, Holmes."

"Stout fellow," said Lewis. He hoped his voice sounded a lot braver than he felt at the moment.

Jenkins had gone inside by the time they finished talking, and Lewis did not see him anywhere about. At noon Mrs Goodring called the two boys in for lunch. She said that Uncle Jonathan and Cousin Pelly were out having a stroll around the grounds, so Bertie and Lewis ate together at a small kitchen table. It was not much of a meal: just some toasted cheese sandwiches and milk, and a small slice of cake each for dessert. After lunch Bertie asked if they might go outside to play, and Mrs Goodring said they could. "Mind you, hurry right back inside if it begins to storm," she said, with an uneasy glance out the window. The clouds still hung unbroken and threatening, and the air fairly hummed with the tension that precedes a really big thunderstorm.

The two boys went outside and circled around the hedge maze. The summer had been hot and dry, Bertie said. The rank grass on the front lawn had died and dried. Now it stood stiff and yellow, a thick sedgy growth that reminded Lewis uncomfortably of the field he had waded through in his nightmares. The brick cottage looked deserted as Bertie and Lewis approached it. The windows were all dark, and no one had bothered to sweep away the pile of dead leaves that had blown up against the front steps. They lay there ankle deep and undisturbed.

"I don't get it," muttered Lewis. "The place looks empty. How long has this Prester guy been living there, anyway?"

Bertie thought back. "A little more than a week," he said. "This is Tuesday. He came a week ago yesterday."

"Well, he hasn't turned on the lights or swept the steps or washed the windows," said Lewis. "In fact, he hasn't done *anything*." They had stopped a few feet from the house. Lewis braced himself. "I'm going to peek through the window," he said.

"Do—do you think you ought?" stammered Bertie.

"I have to," answered Lewis. "You can't do it, and we need to know if he's in there. Be ready to run if I yell. You know which way the Manor is?"

"Sure," said Bertie. "We're on the driveway. You just follow it up until it circles the house."

"OK," said Lewis. "Here goes."

He crept up to the house. The windows were in sad shape, blurred and bleared with layers of ancient grime. He shaded his eyes and peered in through one foggy pane. The house was decidedly gloomy inside, but gradually, as his eyes became accustomed to the dimness, Lewis began to make out shapes. He frowned. The room he was peering into looked unlived-in. A bed, shrouded under a dustcover, stood near the window. Aside from that he could see no furniture at all. A door opposite the window was open and led into a room that looked like a kitchen, with an old-fashioned wood-burning stove just visible. Off to his right was the closed front door. The little cottage appeared to have no other rooms, unless a bathroom lay beyond a closed door to the left of the kitchen. "Empty," Lewis reported to Bertie.

"What now?"

"Well—I vote we knock on the door and see if anyone is home. If he is, you just introduce me and say I am visiting. If not, we'll see if the door is unlocked."

"Lewis!" exclaimed Bertie. "Isn't that breaking and entering?"

"Not if we don't break anything. It's just, uh, entering." Lewis paused. He was not at all positive that he was using proper legal terms, but this was no time to hesitate. He continued: "And besides, we'll just take one quick look and then get out of here."

"Well—all right." But Bertie did not sound happy about the whole idea.

They walked to the front door, where they scuffed through the dead leaves. Lewis tentatively rapped at the door. It gave back a hollow, vacant sound. "Here goes nothing," said Lewis. He reached out to touch the doorknob.

"What's that?" asked Bertie in a sharp, frightened voice.

Lewis had heard it too: a slithery, rustling, creepy noise. It came from the side of the house. He looked and saw the tall, dead grass stirring as if something big were stalking through it, heading for them. "Run!" he yelled.

Bertie broke for the Manor at once, with Lewis right at his heels. Behind them something growled. Lewis cast one terrified glance back when he was halfway to the Manor. The grass beside the drive waved wildly as something huge and invisible bounded through it. Whatever had chased them through the maze at midnight was loose again!

Lewis forced his knees to run harder, faster. His breath burned in his chest. Yet he could barely manage to pull even with Bertie. They came to the circular drive around the house and crossed that—

And Lewis heard a frustrated, low growl from behind. He looked back again. "It stopped!" he panted. Then he remembered the awful night that he and Bertie had stumbled across the same drive. "It can't cross the drive!" he said. "Something is keeping it out!"

Bertie collapsed and lay on his stomach, breathing great ragged gasps of air. Lewis bent over, his hands on his knees. Whatever had chased them had gone. He could barely see the corner of the gatekeeper's cottage down at the foot of the driveway. He blinked, and goosebumps rose on his arms.

A tall, thin man stood beside the house. He had a long, pale face with deep-set eyes, and although Lewis could not clearly see his features, he seemed to be leering in an evil, triumphant way. "Is—is that him?" Lewis panted.

"What?" Bertie asked. "Lewis, you know I can't see!"

"I forgot," apologised Lewis. "There's a skinny man next to—" He broke off in confusion. He had not taken his eyes away from the tall man who stood beside the cottage. And yet the man was gone.

Somehow, even with Lewis staring straight at him, the baleful figure had vanished into thin air.

CHAPTER NINE

As Lewis stared unbelievingly at the place near the cottage where the black-clad man had stood, a hand fell on his shoulder. He jumped a mile and yelped in alarm. Bertie cried out at the same time. But when Lewis turned to see who or what had grabbed him, there stood old Jenkins, a look of reproach on his face. "The master won't like that," said Jenkins, shaking his head. "Runnin' about and makin' an unholy row and all. You and Bertie here ought to be quieter and more considerate of your elders."

"We're sorry, Jenkins," said Bertie. "We had a bit of a fright."

"Oh? And what frightened you two?"

Lewis thought fast. "We were down close to the gatekeeper's cottage, and, uh, we heard a dog or something. It growled at us and we ran up to the house."

Jenkins furrowed his brow and scratched the top of his bald head. "A dog? Nay, there's no dog there, nor any within miles of this place, except for the sheep dogs. And they're too well trained to come mummocking about where they don't belong." Jenkins had not changed back into his suit after working in the garden. He wore overalls and a plaid shirt. He straightened up and gazed down the drive towards the cottage. "You two were best to stay well out of the way of that house, and the man that's staying there. That one's a strange duck, and no mistake."

"Mr Prester, you mean?" asked Bertie.

"Aye, whatever he calls himself," muttered Jenkins. "Needs a rest, he says. Down from

London, he says. A retired businessman, he is—and my sainted Aunt Sarah was a foxtrotting pepperpot! An odd, strange sort of chap, that one. And he comes when I've got the garden on my hands, and the worry of all the chickens dying of the heat or something, and I have the mowing and the painting of the master's bedroom to see to—just when I don't need any extra work."

"He's made you work harder?" asked Lewis.

"Hard enough." Jenkins sniffed in disdain. "All very well for *him* to come tramping down the high road. 'Good afternoon to thee,' he says, like a blessed vicar. 'And may I speak to thy master about a small matter of business?' And him standin' there in the road like a bloomin' scarecrow. 'Speak to him if you want,' said I. 'Though what business the likes of you might have with the master of Barnavelt Manor *I* couldn't guess.' And then the silly goose stood there gapin' at me. 'What are you waiting for?' I asked him, and he says, 'For you to invite me into the house.' Well, that was cheeky. 'Come in, then,' said I, 'and speak more polite-like to the master than you do to me, or it's no business at all you'll be doing with him.'"

Lewis could tell that old Jenkins had taken an instant dislike to the mysterious Mr Prester. "But how did he make you have to work harder?" he asked. "I mean, from what you say, you just had to answer his questions—"

Jenkins scowled down at Lewis. "And wasn't it extra work and trouble for me to have to prowl about the whole blessed Manor to find keys the master never had any call to use before? 'Twasn't the key for the cottage I minded so much. But the other, that nobody had seen for fifty year, that was a bit much. And next morning didn't I have to dust and sweep yon little house to make it fit for his nibs? And then didn't himself show up later that day with a blessed heavy trunk beside him, standin' at the foot of the drive like a bloomin' balloon had set him and it down there? 'Do me the kindness of assisting me with my equipage,' he says, just as cool as you please. I had to lug that heavy trunk in on my poor old back. What did he pack in it? Lead shot and cannonballs? 'Cos that's what it felt like, and me with lumbago too!"

Bertie frowned in concentration. He pushed his green spectacles back into place on his sweaty nose. "Uh, what was the other key you had to find?"

Jenkins sniffed again. "Never you mind, Bertie Goodring. But I warn the two of you: leave yon cottage alone, and give precious Mr Matthew Prester a wide berth. He'll bring no good to this old house, mark my words."

Lewis and Bertie went back around to the rear of the house, where a big garage housed only Cousin Pelly's ridiculous little Austin Seven, though it had space enough for half a dozen more cars. "What key do you suppose Jenkins was looking for?" Bertie asked.

Lewis had to admit that he had no idea. "But you know what?" he added. "I'll bet you could find out what it was."

"Me?" Bertie sounded surprised but interested.

"Sure," said Lewis. "What does anyone do when they look for stuff that they haven't seen in ages and ages? They go to everybody else and say, 'Have you seen my left-handed monkey wrench?' or whatever it is. They do that even if they know the other person has never seen the whatchamacallit—"

Bertie nodded in comprehension. "I see," he said.

Just then they heard Bertie's mother calling him. "Crikey," said Bertie. "What time is it, Lewis?"

Lewis looked at his wristwatch. "Just two o'clock," he said. "Why?"

"I have to go. It's time for my lessons."

Lewis felt scandalised. "Don't you get a summer holiday?"

"No, not when my mum is the teacher," said Bertie. "Gotta go."

"Hey," said Lewis. "Be sure to ask your mother about the key. I'll bet you anything Jenkins came to her and asked her if she'd seen it."

"Will do," said Bertie, and he trotted off.

As soon as he had gone, Lewis began to feel uneasy and anxious, as if some danger he only half sensed lurked in his vicinity. The air was even damper and warmer than it had been earlier, and he decided to go inside. The old manor house felt deserted. From some distant room a big clock ticked heavily. Lewis did not feel like sitting alone in his room, and he certainly did not feel like scouting around on his own. He decided to go back to the library, Master Martin's study. Maybe he could find a good book there. He slipped into the room and felt somehow better. Some places just have a good feeling that certain people can recognise. This study was just such a place, in Lewis's opinion.

He browsed for some minutes before he struck pure gold. A whole shelf of books, bound in black, had the title *The Strand* stamped upon them, and various years beneath that, all of them in the 1890s and early 1900s. Lewis pulled one of these out at random and opened it. He saw immediately that the books were bound volumes of a magazine. The volume that he held covered part of the year 1892. He turned a few pages and then grinned. He was looking at a picture of Sherlock Holmes and Dr Watson sitting in a railway car, very much like the one he and his uncle had ridden from London. The drawing illustrated one of his favourite Sherlock Holmes stories, "Silver Blaze." Lewis realised that this was the magazine in which Sir Arthur Conan Doyle had first published his tales of the master detective. And though he had read all the stories before, Lewis always liked to renew old acquaintances. He took the bound magazine back to his room and lost himself in the world of Victorian England.

Several hours passed, and then someone knocked tentatively. Lewis closed the book and went to answer the door. Bertie stood there, and he was fairly bursting with news. "I know what the key was," he whispered.

"Come on in," said Lewis. He looked up and down the hall, but no one else was in sight.

Still, he carefully closed the door. "OK," he said. "So what key was Jenkins hunting?"

"He asked Mum if she had any idea where the key to the lumber room might be," said Bertie. "And then later he said he had found it in the odds-and-ends drawer of the scullery."

"So what is this lumber room?" asked Lewis. The name conjured up visions of circular saws, hammers, and nails.

"It's a storage room," answered Bertie. "It's high up in this wing of the house, above the top story."

"Oh—an attic," said Lewis. "Let's see what's there. I don't think Cousin Pelly and Uncle Jonathan are back yet."

"Well, all right," said Bertie with some hesitation. "But Mum wouldn't like me poking about up there, so do let's be quiet."

Pelly and his household lived in only the east wing of the rambling old manor house, and even in this wing they occupied only the ground and first floors. The second and third floors were as empty and unused as the main body of the old house. The stairs opened into a very dark hallway, lighted by only one small, round window. At the far end of the hallway, next to the window, a narrow door opened on to another staircase. This one was so dusty and close that it gave Lewis an attack of sneezing, which he tried to stifle.

The two friends crept up the narrow stairs as carefully as they could, but the dry wood creaked beneath their feet all the same. Lewis found it hard going. The hall had been murky enough, but total darkness shrouded this stairway. The doorway behind them was only a dusky opening, and up ahead Lewis could see only a thin, dim line where the door at the top of the stairs did not quite fit in the door frame. He found the handle by feel and gave it an experimental twist. The latch squeaked with rust, but the handle moved, and the door swung inwards.

It was an attic, all right. The air was hot in their faces, and it had that closed-in, dusty smell that only attic rooms get. The ceiling overhead sloped at a sharp angle, and the beams were hung with dusty cobwebs swaying lazily in the faint breeze from the open door. Two of the very narrow arrow-slot windows let a little light into the place. Lewis saw a clutter of broken furniture and paintings wrapped in old sheets and boxes furry with undisturbed layers of dust. Lewis stepped cautiously into the room. "Something has been taken," he said.

"How do you know?" asked Bertie.

"The floor is about an inch deep in dust," replied Lewis, exaggerating only a little. "But right there against the wall there is a clear space, about two feet by three. Something rectangular has rested there until recently. Something like a big box—or maybe a trunk."

"Mr Prester had a trunk," said Bertie.

"I remember," murmured Lewis. "Hello, what's this?" He stooped and picked up something. It was a book. A very old book, from the fuzzy, crumbly feel of the leather binding. And he saw that on the floor beneath where the book had lain, the dust rested in an

unbroken layer. That meant the book had been dropped very recently.

"What did you find?" Bertie wanted to know.

"It's a thin book," said Lewis. "Now, this is strange. In fact—"

From far down below, a high-pitched voice interrupted him: "Boys! I say, boys! Confound you two young scoundrels, where are you?"

"Mr Barnavelt," gasped Bertie. "And he sounds ever so angry!"

"Let's go," said Lewis. He pulled up his shirt and slipped the book down inside the waistband of his trousers. Then he tugged his shirt back into place, hoping that the outline of the book would not show. He and Bertie hurried downstairs, carefully closing doors behind them.

They found Pelly standing at the bottom of the stairs on the ground floor. "There you are," he said, sounding irritable. "Looking all over for you. What have you been up to, eh?"

"Uh, Bertie was just showing me around," said Lewis. "I thought it would be all right, Cousin Pelly. I'm sorry if—"

A terrific roll of thunder cut him off, and he flinched. A moment later rain began to pound hard against the house. Pelly threw his head back and took a deep breath. "What a storm!" he said. "This is going to be a glorious night, my boys. I wouldn't want you to miss it!"

Something in his tone made the words ominous. Bertie had to hurry off to help his mother close windows, and Lewis slipped away to go back to his own bedroom. He wanted to look at the odd, slim volume he had smuggled down. And he wanted to think about the curious observation he had made in the attic room.

Though someone had obviously taken the trunk or box from its place against the wall and carried it all the way across the room, the floor had lain in an unbroken film of dust. Not one footprint disturbed it. How could anyone cross over that floor and leave no mark?

No one could. At least, thought Lewis, no one *human*.

CHAPTER TEN

Dinner was cheerless. Outside the Manor the summer storm raged, bringing on an early twilight. The wind moaned, thunder rattled the glass in the windows, and rain pelted down so hard that it sounded like pebbles clattering on the roof. Just as Jonathan, Pelly, and Lewis were finishing their meal, an especially loud crash of thunder shook the house. A moment later the lights went out, plunging the dining room into gloom. "Ah," said Pelly. "Lightning's downed the wires, I expect. Never mind! Candles will do. They lighted this old house for centuries before Father had the place wired for electricity."

Mrs Goodring brought three tall white candles in, each in its own holder, and Pelly lit one. Lewis did not like the way the yellow light made his cousin's face look. With the candle shining up from beneath, his features took on a sharp, predatory expression. The good-humoured eyes became narrow and sly, and the friendly, wrinkled face seemed frozen in a savage grimace. Lewis was happy enough to take one of the candles and find his way to his bedroom.

He had not had time to examine the thin book he had brought down from the lumber room. When Cousin Pelly had told him to get ready for dinner, Lewis had hastily thrust the slim volume under his pillow. Now Lewis set the candle on the small desk at the head of his bed, and in its subdued illumination he got undressed. He donned his favourite pyjamas, the maroon pair with bright-red buttons and trim. Then he took the flickering candle to the bathroom down the hall, where he brushed his teeth. That done, Lewis returned to his bedroom, locked the door behind him, and got into bed. The wind still whistled against the windows, and spatters of rain clashed against the panes with fitful violence. Lewis shivered and reached beneath his pillow. The book was still there, right beside the trusty torch. Although he had replaced the worn-out batteries, Lewis decided not to use the torch for reading. The candle would do, and he wanted to save the torch in case of emergencies.

Lewis had never tried to read by candlelight, and at first he found it difficult. The illumination was dim and yellow and wavering, making the letters on the page dance slowly before his eyes. The book proved to be a handwritten diary, and the writing was very old-fashioned and hard to read. The letters looped and scrawled and squiggled across the page, and the ink had faded to a rusty brown. Since the brittle old paper had taken on a deep tan colour with age, the writing on the pages looked dim and faint. The cover of the book bore no title, so Lewis studied the flyleaf of the diary for a long time before he was really sure what the writing said:

The Persecution, for Witch-Craft,
of Martin Christian Barnavelt
Writ by Himself, *Anno* 1688

Lewis struggled through the first few pages, and gradually he learned how to interpret the old-fashioned handwriting more easily. His eyes grew round as he read old Martin Barnavelt's story, "writ by himself." The book began, "I, Martin Christian Barnavelt, finding myself growing old and infirm, am determin'd to set this Account down for Posterity, that in future Years, my Descendants may understand and know the Truth behind the false, vicious, and wicked Accusations brought against me." The sentences were all like that, long and rambling and swimming with commas like schools of little black tadpoles. Still, the story told by the antique writing was a version of the tale different from the others Lewis had heard or read. It even differed very widely from the privately printed book done by Martin Barnavelt's own son.

Lewis gathered from the book that Malachiah Pruitt's witch-finding had hurt a good many people, not just Lewis's ancestor. Martin wrote that he had witnessed Witch Finder Pruitt's persecution of "two poore harmless Women of the County, both Widows, and both doubtless innocent of any Evil whatever." The fact that old Pruitt had taken over Barnavelt Manor and held his witchcraft trials there especially irritated Martin. "If these poor Souls confess'd the practice of the Black Arts, then who among us would not, if tormented by the devilish Machines, that Witch Finder Pruitt had install'd in my Cellars?" Martin asked at one point.

Then the book took a sinister turn. At first Martin merely explained what had happened to the two poor women: how Pruitt had brought them to trial for conjuring and for having "familiar spirits" in the form of a cat and a toad. But Pruitt was not both judge and jury. A panel of "sober and decorous Men" sat as the jury, and before they would condemn the women to death, these jurors insisted on convincing evidence. This they got, Martin wrote, when "Signs and Wonders, of undoubted Magick, did appear; *viz.*, the Moving of Objects, without any visible Hand, the Cuffing and Scratching of certain of the Men, by an invisible Animal or Sprite, and divers other Marvels."

At first the scary events took even Martin in, and he was ready to believe that the women were witches, even though they wept and protested their innocence. Then a darker explanation occurred to him. "Once when the Confusion reign'd, of some invisible Spirit groaning and trampling and making other Sounds, I kept a close Watch upon the Witch Finder. I saw him make certain Gestures and Movements of a mystical Significance; and so I came to understand, that Witch Finder Pruitt was himself the Wizard. But he did become aware that I watch'd him, and so he determin'd to make me his next Victim, and so gain a Hold on Barnavelt Manor forever."

Lewis frowned as he read the next few pages. They made one thing very clear: Martin Barnavelt was far from ignorant of magic and enchantment. He wrote that Malachiah Pruitt used a spell called "The Summoning of Invisible Servants," a true act of evil sorcery. "The Villain then sent forth these airy and insubstantial Spirits," wrote Martin, "to deceive Witnesses into the Belief, that the poor innocent Women he accus'd, did work those Wonders that the Jury took as Proof." However, Martin had no way of proving that, and soon Pruitt ordered Martin himself imprisoned under a charge of witchcraft. Pruitt had him locked up in a cellar room of the Manor, where Martin came close to despair. Fortunately, one of Martin's servants brought him his meals. The accused wizard sounded out this man, and he found that the servant still felt a great loyalty to him. "I ventur'd then to ask this good Fellow," wrote Martin, "to bring unto me a Charm of great goodness and power, *viz.*, the Amulet of Constantine. He found Occasion to take it from my Study, and to convey it privily to my Cell. There I perform'd the necessary Incantations—"

Lewis blinked. Old Martin Barnavelt had been a wizard, after all! But then, Jonathan Barnavelt was a wizard, and his magic had always been harmless and good. Somehow Lewis felt that Martin had been the same kind of magician, and not a servant of evil. He read on. The Amulet of Constantine, whatever that was, had the power to undo evil enchantments and to break malevolent spells. Martin was too late to save the lives of the poor women, whom Pruitt had hanged, but he did accomplish something. On the morning of his trial, Martin had used the Amulet to cast a spell that would "break off Witch Finder Pruitt's hold on the evil Spirit, which aided him, and to lock that Spirit away in a close, secret Place." That morning, Malachiah Pruitt appeared at the trial ailing and weak. And when he had tried some of his magical gestures and passes, he fell to the floor in a dead faint, from which he never recovered.

"Speechless and helpless he remain'd from

that Day," wrote Martin. "Bereft of his dire Enchantments, Witch Finder Pruitt aged at an ungodly rate, changing from a Man of five-and-forty to one of five Score in two short Years. And so at last he died and pass'd away, and the World was rid of a very wicked Scoundrel."

The last pages of the account were extremely terse. Martin briefly explained that Charles II, the new King who ascended the throne in 1660, had betrayed him. "It pleas'd certain Members of the Court, to whisper to his Majesty that I was one of the detested Pruitt's Helpers and Friends. The King chose to believe them, and the Crown prevented me from regaining Barnavelt Manor for long, weary years." Angry at what the new King had done, Martin felt justified in keeping for himself "one of that malefactor Pruitt's gaudy Toys, giv'n him for his Part in the ignoble Slaughter of King Charles I." He added that, "Now growing old, I fear for the Security of the Place where I immur'd that evil Spirit. And so, I have caus'd a Tomb of Brick to be rais'd above that spot, and with my own Hands I have fix'd the Amulet, with its Chain wrapp'd about that wicked Pruitt's most priz'd Toy, in the Lid of this Tomb. There may its righteous Power keep the corrupt Spirit captive forever."

Lewis caught his breath. So that was what he had released from the brick vault! No wonder it had frightened him and Bertie so badly—if the book told the story correctly, the invisible creature was a spirit of darkest malice. And maybe Martin Barnavelt's diary had given him a way of fighting that spirit. Lewis shivered. His candle had burned to a drippy stump, and the wind and rain had died down. Lewis came to a decision. He would have to tell Uncle Jonathan about what he had discovered. He did not want to admit what he had done, but neither could he bear to face the idea of fighting this terrible thing alone. He got out of bed and reached for the candle.

A terrific blast of lightning and an immediate explosion of thunder made him cry out. He dropped the candle, and the fall snuffed out the flame. Lewis stood in darkness, his ears ringing and his heart thudding painfully. He was looking towards one of the bedroom windows, but he could see only a lingering blob of greenish light.

Then the formless blob took on a shape. Lewis gasped. It was not just an after-image. A *face* floated eerily outside the window, looking in at him. A lean, leering face with deep-set eyes. A face that looked like the awful skull-moon that had glared down on him in the maze. The man in black was floating in air just outside his window!

Lewis opened his mouth to shout. He dimly saw two long, bony hands weaving an intricate gesture in the air. The book in his hand grew hot. A cloud of black smoke suddenly gushed from it, choking and evil smelling. He threw the book away from him, and in mid-air it burst into flame. It burned to nothing in a *poof,* and Lewis heard triumphant laughter ringing in his mind. Lewis's head spun, and he fell to the floor unconscious.

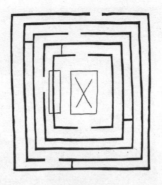

CHAPTER ELEVEN

Thin morning sunlight woke Lewis. He lay on the floor with his cheek against the frayed carpet of his bedroom. He felt cold and achy, and for a few puzzled moments he could not understand why he lay on the floor and not in bed. Then the terrifying memory of that spectral, grinning face came back to him, and he jumped up. Lewis looked wildly around for the diary of Martin Barnavelt—and then remembered that it had exploded into some kind of supernatural flame. He could not even see any ashes. Then he steeled himself and looked out the window.

Everything appeared perfectly normal. The morning sun shone through a high, hazy layer of milky-white clouds. Scattered across the side lawn lay sodden twigs and leaves, ripped off the trees by the previous evening's storm. Lewis opened the window, put his head out, and looked down. The drop from his casement to the ground was sheer, without even a ledge for anyone to stand on. The face at his window had belonged to someone—or *something*—that could float in mid-air. Lewis remembered a line from a play that he, Jonathan, Rose Rita, and Mrs Zimmermann had attended in Ann Arbor in Michigan one evening back in the spring:

Fair is foul, and foul is fair:
Hover through the fog and filthy air.

The play had been *Macbeth,* and the characters speaking the lines were the three hideous witches. Lewis thought that William Shakespeare had such creatures sized up about right.

He knew he had to do something. The best course would have been to show the diary to his uncle and to confess what he and Bertie had accidentally done out in the maze. With the diary gone, he could only hope that Jonathan would believe him. Lewis had to admit that in the light of day, the story sounded pretty wild, even to him. Still, Uncle Jonathan had learned a certain kind of magic himself, and he was the current treasurer of the Capharnaum County Magicians Society, so maybe it would not be impossible to convince him that some diabolic enchantment was at work. Lewis dressed himself and went to the door that opened into his uncle's bedroom. He tapped very softly on the door. Then when no one answered, he knocked louder.

Still no answer. Lewis tried the doorknob, and the door swung inwards. He went into his uncle's room. Everything was just as Jonathan had left it: the nightstand held his pipe and pipe cleaners, embroidered tobacco pouch, wallet, pocket watch with its paper-clip chain, fat black fountain pen, and torch. Jonathan's big, battered suitcase rested on a stand at the foot of the bed. The closet door stood open, and Lewis could see Jonathan's clothes hanging there. The bedclothes were rumpled, as if the bed had been slept in, and the pillow still held the impression of Jonathan's head.

But Jonathan Barnavelt was nowhere to be found.

Growing uneasy, Lewis went downstairs. Perhaps Uncle Jonathan and Cousin Pelly were having breakfast. No, the dining room was quiet and empty. Lewis forced himself to look out the windows at the front lawn. The hedge maze was not stirring, but the pale morning light made it grim and dark, with deep green shadows under the overgrown branches. Lewis went back towards the kitchen. He noticed that he was walking on his tiptoes. The hallway lay in darkness, but when he touched a light switch, nothing happened. The power was still out.

Lewis timidly opened the kitchen door. Mrs Goodring sat immobile at the table, with her hands folded in her lap. She was staring straight ahead at the stove. As Lewis came in, her head slowly turned towards him. The movement struck Lewis as weird, because her shoulders did not change position at all. Her head simply came around, like a mechanical doll's. "What do *you* want?" she asked him. Her eyes were distant and cold.

Lewis swallowed. "I—I was looking for my uncle," he murmured.

For a moment Mrs Goodring simply stared. Then, with absolutely no expression in her face or voice, she said, "Mr Barnavelt and your uncle have gone away on a short trip. You are to be in my care until they return."

"Oh," said Lewis. "Uh—is Bertie anywhere around?"

"Bertie?" snapped Mrs Goodring, as if she had never heard the name before. She was quiet for another moment, and then she said, "My son cannot play with you today. Why not go outside? There is a funny maze you can play in all by yourself." She smiled at him, but her smile looked all wrong. It looked like the snarl an angry dog turns on an enemy, with nothing friendly in it.

No one had to tell Lewis that something was terribly wrong with Mrs Goodring. He tried to return her smile, but his face felt frozen. "Uh, no, thanks. It's, uh, probably still too wet from all the rain. I think I'll just read in my room." When Mrs Goodring did not reply, Lewis asked, "Do you think I can have some breakfast, please?"

Her head swivelled back around in that weird way, and she stood up from the table. She marched stiffly over to a cabinet. She opened this door and that, as if she had no idea where the food could be. She found a loaf of home-baked bread and put that on the table. Then she wandered to the icebox, which she had some trouble opening. She took out a pitcher of milk and put it on the table beside the bread. Then she sat down again, staring straight ahead.

"Uh, thanks," Lewis said. He found the silverware in a drawer and got a plate and glass for himself from a shelf above the icebox. Although he had almost no appetite, he cut himself a slice of bread, buttered it, and ate it, washing it down with a glass of milk. Then he put the food and milk away and rinsed the dishes in the sink. Mrs Goodring did not even look his way as he left the kitchen.

Lewis hurried back up to his uncle's bedroom. He opened the suitcase and looked at the clothes there. Then he checked the closet. The shirt and trousers that his uncle had worn the day before lay on the floor of the closet. The red vest and tweed jacket hung neatly on the rack, along with clean trousers and shirts. As far as Lewis could tell, Jonathan had not dressed to go out. Something was very much amiss.

He went back to his room and burrowed through his suitcase until he came up with the little pocket notebook where he had written Constable Dwiggins's address. He carried this downstairs. The telephone rested on a tall round table at the foot of the stairs. It was the old-fashioned kind called a candlestick phone, the type whose tall mouthpiece you hold in one hand and the earpiece in the other. It did not even have a dial. Lewis picked it up and clattered the earpiece hook up and down three or four times, the way he had seen people do in movies. An operator answered.

Speaking softly, Lewis said, "I have to get in touch with Police Constable Henry Dwiggins, in London. I don't know his telephone number, but this is his address." And he read off the street and number.

"I will try to reach him," said the operator. For a few seconds the line buzzed and crackled. Then Lewis heard the phone ringing on the other end. It was a funny sound, not like an American phone at all. This made a noise more like a small robot gargling.

"Hello, yes?" said a woman's pleasant, elderly voice.

"Uh, I'm calling Police Constable Henry Dwiggins," said Lewis.

"What? Henry? He is my son, but he is on duty just now. May I tell him who called?"

"Yes," said Lewis. "This is Lewis Barnavelt. I need help. Please tell him I am at Barnavelt Manor, near the village of Dinsdale in West Sussex. Should I repeat that?"

No one answered. The line sounded dead. Lewis clicked the receiver hook up and down several times, but no one responded. He had no idea how much of his message had got through, or if any at all had. He had the creepy feeling that someone *knew* he was trying to telephone the police and was playing with him, the way a cat might play with a mouse.

"I gotta go for help," Lewis told himself. He went outside. The sun had not yet risen very high, and the day was cool and damp. Lewis hesitated for a few moments, but then he strode off down the driveway. He figured he could walk to the village in less than an hour. Surely there would be a policeman in Dinsdale who would listen to him. He carefully kept as far away from the hedge maze as he could, but when the gatekeeper's cottage came in sight, Lewis stopped as if paralysed. A figure dressed in black stopped beside one of the gateposts, bent over, and fooled with something. Then the figure straightened up. With a gasp of relief, Lewis recognised the bald dome of old Jenkins.

He hurried on down. What was Jenkins doing? As he got closer, Lewis saw that the manservant had looped a heavy chain around one of the gateposts and had secured it with a padlock. Now he stretched the chain across the drive and fastened it around the other post with a small steel hook. The chain clanked and clattered as it swung back and forth. Jenkins was sealing off the drive!

The servant turned suddenly and stared at Lewis. His eyes had that same awful emptiness that Lewis had seen in Mrs Goodring's vacant gaze. Lewis edged on towards the road. He could duck under the chain and run towards town—

Jenkins lifted his right hand and pointed his finger at Lewis. "Nay, thou sprout of a cursed Barnavelt," he said in a strange voice. "Thou'lt not flee by this path. Get thee back to the place of judgement! Thy doom waits for thee!"

Lewis's nerve broke. He turned and ran back to the Manor as fast as he could go. He had heard that mocking, hollow voice before. It sounded just like the tone he had heard in his head when he had imagined the skull-faced moon was talking to him. Or *had* he imagined it?

Lewis felt like bursting into tears. He sensed that invisible eyes watched him secretly, with gloating triumph. He was afraid to try to run away, and he was afraid to go back into the Manor. When he got to the point where the drive curved to run around the house, Lewis paused and chanced a look back towards the gate. Jenkins stood there, as stiff as a statue, his pointing arm still extended. And something flickered momentarily at the window of the gatekeeper's cottage. Could it be the same repulsive face that had looked in his window during the storm? Lewis feared that it was.

At a loss, he decided to go back inside and up to his room after all. He had to think this through. Everything pointed to an appalling conclusion: Mrs Goodring and Jenkins were hypnotised or brainwashed. His uncle had been taken from his room in the night. His cousin Pelly was also missing.

And Lewis was a prisoner in Barnavelt Manor.

CHAPTER TWELVE

Inside Barnavelt Manor, Lewis found Mrs Goodring waiting for him with that same empty, mindless gaze. "Don't you think you had better go to your room?" she asked. After a moment's pause, she repeated, "Don't you think you had better go to your room?" in exactly the same way. Lewis did not speak to her, but he did climb the stairs. He heard a sound behind and looked back. Mrs Goodring was coming up after him, with the monotonous slow tread of a zombie. "Don't you think you had better go to your room?" she asked again.

Lewis thought he would come down with the screaming meemies if he heard that question again. He hurried to his bedroom and closed the door. He paced the floor for several minutes. Then he tiptoed to the door and pulled it open slowly and quietly, until he could just peek out the crack. Mrs Goodring stood motionless in the hall, her unblinking eyes staring in his direction. Lewis closed the door again and locked it. After a moment he hauled the chair over to the door and tilted it back, bracing it under the handle. He felt safer with the door barred as well as locked. He latched the door that led into his uncle's room too, and pulled the desk over to hold that one closed.

He looked at his watch. It was just past nine o'clock. How could he get a message through to the outside world? He wondered if whatever had happened to Mrs Goodring and Jenkins had also happened to everyone else. Was Uncle Jonathan shambling about somewhere in the Manor like Frankenstein's monster? Was Cousin Pelly one of those glassy-eyed automatons? Lewis might be the only one in the whole house still in his right mind! The thought terrified him. He wasn't just scared now. He felt a deep, gnawing horror, and a sense of hopelessness. Who was he kidding when he played Sherlock Holmes? Just himself, that was all. He wasn't a brave, brilliant detective. He was just a lonely boy with an overactive imagination and a deep desire to be bigger and stronger and smarter than he was.

But he couldn't give up. Not now. Not when he could be the only one capable of bringing help. And yet he knew Mrs Goodring still stood guard outside his room. How to elude her?

Lewis went to the window again. It still stood open. He put his head out and looked straight down. It was twenty feet to the ground—and the ground looked hard, even after the soaking rains. If he only had a ladder—

"Sherlock Holmes would *make* a ladder," said Lewis aloud. He turned to the bed. He was still frightened, but now he was feeling another emotion. He had become angry. Angry at the horrible old witch finder who somehow had brought this terror on him and Pelly and Uncle Jonathan and the other victims over all those centuries. Angry at the feeling that some invisible spirit was watching him and gloating because it thought he was so dumb and it was so darned smart. Well, two can play at that game!

Lewis threw off the coverlet and then stripped the blanket and both sheets from his bed. He knotted these all together, and then he pushed and grunted and groaned until he had shoved the bed up against the wall next to the open window. He quickly tied a corner of the blanket to the bedpost, and then he tossed the improvised rope of blanket and sheets out the opening. He leaned out and peered down. Not too bad. The bottom sheet dangled about eight feet above the ground, but that was lots better than twenty.

Lewis got his torch and jammed it into the waistband of his corduroy pants. He grabbed his Sherlock Holmes hat and crammed it beneath his belt. Then he climbed on to the windowsill and tugged at the blanket. What if it gave way? If the knots slipped, he could be killed or paralysed for life. It was a stupid thing to attempt, he knew, but he felt desperate. "Don't think about it," muttered Lewis to himself. He took a deep breath and let himself slip through the window. He clutched his makeshift rope so tightly that his fingers ached. For a dizzy second he was so scared that he could not even make his hands loosen their desperate clench. Then he forced his muscles to relax. He slipped down the blanket, inch by inch, until he got to the first knot. The sheet was easier to hold on to than the thick blanket. He let himself slide down a little faster. At last he dangled from the end of the last sheet. His arms ached fiercely, but his swinging feet could not touch the ground. Lewis was afraid to look down, but he forced himself.

He had been holding his breath. He let it out in a gust of relief. His toes swayed only two feet above the ground. Lewis let go and dropped to earth. The wet sod squished under the impact and threw him off balance, but he managed not to fall down. He was free, at least for the moment.

What now? Lewis considered. He would give anything for some help and encouragement. He needed Bertie, but he had no idea what had happened to his friend. Maybe the evil spirit had put him under its spell, but what if Bertie was all right? All right, but a captive, as he had been? He made up his mind and stole around to the back of the Manor, keeping close to the wall and ducking down low to creep under the windows he passed. At the corner he saw something that explained why his telephone call had been interrupted. The telephone wire came out of the house there, and someone had cut it. Whoever had snipped the connection had made sure that the wires could not be easily connected, because a section at least six inches long had been cut away.

At the corner Lewis looked around nervously, but no one was in sight. He remembered that

Bertie's bedroom window looked out at the vegetable garden. He decided that to have that particular angle of view, Bertie's window had to be the second one from the corner. He sneaked to that window and, raising his head, cautiously peered inside.

He had chosen the right window. Bertie lay face down on his bed, with his arms folded under his head. He looked as if he had been crying. Lewis tapped quietly on the window, making no more noise than a fly might make if it flew head-on into the glass.

Bertie's head came up. He groped for his green spectacles, put them on, and came over to the window. He opened it a crack. "Who's there?" he whispered.

"The game's afoot," breathed Lewis. If old Growly had taken over Bertie's mind, then that phrase would be meaningless. But if Bertie was himself—

"I shall be with you in a moment, Holmes," said Bertie. "Lewis? This window sticks rather badly, but if we both try, we might manage it."

They shoved and tugged at the window sash until they had it open just far enough for Bertie to worm out. Lewis helped him. "Where can we go that's private?" whispered Lewis.

"The toolshed next to the garage," answered Bertie promptly. "No one's ever there unless Jenkins has to work on the car."

"Come on, then."

The toolshed was a little addition on one side of the huge garage. As they approached it, Lewis saw that Cousin Pelly's boxy old car still rested in its place. It had not budged an inch since he had noticed it there the day before. Uncle Jonathan and Cousin Pelly have gone on a short trip, he thought. Like fun, they have. The two boys crept into the shed and closed the door. A row of small, square windows very high up in one wall let daylight into the narrow little room. The wall beneath the windows had rows and rows of pegs, and all sorts of things hung on them: red rubber inner tubes plastered all over with patches, coils of copper wire, and broken fan belts unravelling into long hanks of black fibres. A narrow shelf ran along the other wall, with open cabinets underneath holding shallow wooden boxes filled with tools. "What's going on, Lewis?" asked Bertie.

Lewis hopped up to sit on the shelf. "I don't really know," he admitted. "But I have a few ideas, only they're kind of horrible." He quickly told Bertie about the diary and what it had revealed about old Malachiah Pruitt. He hesitated for a few seconds, but then reflected that he owed the whole truth to Bertie. He breathed deeply and rushed on to add, "And there's something else too. Malachiah Pruitt was the evil sorcerer, but Martin Barnavelt was also a wizard. A good one. I know that sounds crazy, but—but—Bertie, there are such things. I know. Uncle Jonathan is a good wizard too." There. He'd said it.

"What can he do?" asked Bertie, sounding interested.

"Well, he can eclipse the moon, and create illusions," said Lewis. "And he can make the neighbour's cat whistle songs. But none of that can help us now. And I thought you didn't believe in witches and stuff, anyway."

Bertie's expression was grave. "I didn't, but you say that Jonathan is a wizard, so he must be one. I guess I was wrong, that's all."

"Don't tell anyone about this," cautioned Lewis. "Uncle Jonathan wouldn't like anyone to know. It's kind of a family secret, and I've gotta trust you now that I've spilled it."

"I won't tell, honour bright," said Bertie. Somehow Lewis knew he could believe him. The blind boy was silent for a minute, and then he asked, "What can we do, Lewis? Something awful has come over Mum. She acted quite cross with me this morning for no reason at all, and she told me I had to stay in my room all day. I think something is wrong with her."

"Boy, is it ever. Bertie, I believe that whatever we let out of that vault has some sort of spell over your mum, and over Jenkins too," said Lewis in a grim voice. "Worst of all, I don't know what we can do to help. The only thing

I know to try is to make a run for it. But I have a rotten feeling that once we get outside the circular drive, the spirit or demon or whatever it is will be right on our heels."

"What about the amulet you read about in the book?" asked Bertie. "If it has power to bind evil spirits, maybe it has power to chase them away too. "

Lewis sat up straighter. "Yeah," he said. "I hadn't even thought about that, but you're right. If this Amulet of Constantine could hold that nasty critter down for three hundred years, I'll bet it could snap Jenkins and your mum right out of their trance. It might even help us send the invisible servant back to wherever it came from in the first place."

"We've got to try for it, then."

"But it's buried in the vault," objected Lewis. "How are we supposed to get it out?"

"We *are* in a toolshed," Bertie pointed out in a reasonable voice.

"So we are," said Lewis. He saw the plan right away, but after a moment he had to confess, "Bertie, I don't know if I can go through with this. I'm scared."

After a moment Bertie mumbled softly, "I am too."

"I know you are. But I guess you're right—we gotta try. We'll have to make a run for it once we get into the maze. You think you can get us to the stone bench fast?"

"I ought to be able to do that," replied Bertie. "I've been through the maze a hundred times, at least."

"OK." Lewis frowned in concentration. "Let's see if we can find some hammers and chisels and crowbars. Somehow I don't think old Growly will be back in that centre clearing where the vault is."

"Why not?"

"Well, if *you* had been locked up in a dark little room for three hundred years, and then got out, would you wait there to get shoved inside again?"

"That makes sense," admitted Bertie.

"So I think if we can get there fast, it'll be

OK. According to that diary, Martin Barnavelt sealed the amulet in the lid. I'd bet you anything that it's under that dome right in the middle. And if we can break open the dome, and the amulet is inside, then—then we'll decide what to do next," Lewis finished lamely.

Bertie could offer no better plan. Lewis soon found a sturdy ball-peen hammer, a tarnished but heavy metal chisel, and a short crowbar. He gave the latter to Bertie, and he carried the other tools himself. For luck he pulled his Sherlock Holmes hat out of his belt and tugged it on. "Let's go," he said. "We're as ready as we'll ever be."

The boys saw no sign of Jenkins. They crept around front until they stood at the top of the slope—about twenty yards from the hedge maze. But to get to it, they would have to step off the circular drive. Both Bertie and Lewis were quite convinced by now that some magic beneath the drive warded off the invisible servant. Getting up the nerve to move past that boundary was like building up the courage to jump off a high diving board. At first you thought you could never do it, and then you imagined how awful it would be, and then suddenly you stepped off into thin air and were on your way. Both Bertie and Lewis leaped forward at the same moment.

Bertie had one hand on Lewis's elbow. Lewis had to watch out for both of them, choosing a path that wouldn't let Bertie trip over a root or a stone. They were at the entrance to the maze before he knew it, and they plunged right in. Lewis gritted his teeth. The air had a strange feeling again, like the tension building up in the atmosphere before a bolt of lightning. If they could just reach that bench—

They twisted and turned and twisted again, with Bertie taking the lead now. Something rattled in the hedges far behind them, maybe just a bird. It made them both move faster all the same. "Around this corner," panted Bertie, and sure enough, there was the mossy bench.

Bertie threw himself on the ground and crawled under the stone bench, and half a second later Lewis wriggled through the opening too. They collapsed, breathing hard and listening for sounds of pursuit. A bird twittered somewhere. The wind rustled in the hedges. They heard nothing else.

"I think this is a safety zone," said Lewis when he had caught his breath. "It may be the one blind spot that old Growly has."

"Let's get to work," replied Bertie. "I don't want to leave my mum in the power of that thing."

Lewis hoisted himself up to the stone lid of the brick vault. He noticed that things had changed. Little twigs lay here and there on the lid, and a black beetle trundled along on some beetly mission. Before, the vault clearing had shown no signs of life, and no fallen leaves at all had lain in it. Since the evil spirit had escaped and gone outside, everything seemed to be returning to normal in the heart of the maze. Lewis braced the chisel against the side of the dome and pounded it with the hammer. The blows made a kind of metallic music: *clang*!

clang! *clang*! The sound reminded Lewis of "The Anvil Chorus," a tune he had heard played in a hundred cartoons. Chips of stone flaked off and flew away. Lewis wondered what would happen if one of those things hit his eye. It would blind him, probably. He squinted and half averted his face.

Another blow, and another, and suddenly the chisel sank a couple of inches through the dome's surface. "Got it!" Lewis said. "Gimme the crowbar."

He worked the curved end of the bar into the little slot he had chiselled. Then he and Bertie tugged hard on the straight end of the bar, applying all the leverage they could. *Sproin-n-ng*! A big chunk of the dome peeled back. Lewis could see now that the dome had a lining of greenish metal. Probably old Martin had put a copper bowl upside down and plastered a thin layer of stone over that. The copper had corroded and weakened over the centuries, and now it offered no resistance. Seeing a hole as broad as the palm of his hand now open in the dome, Lewis took the hammer and smacked away. He split off large fragments, and in a moment he was able to reach inside. He pulled out a wooden box a little bigger and deeper than a cigar box, with hinges and a lock made of badly tarnished brass.

"We don't have time to worry about finding a key," Lewis said with a grunt. He stuck the chisel under the edge of the lid and pried. The old hinges gave way with a screech of metal, and the box practically fell to pieces in his hand.

"What is it, Lewis?" asked Bertie anxiously. "Is the Amulet there?"

"It sure is," said Lewis. "And something else too."

He held a surprisingly heavy object in his hand. Wrapped around it was a gold chain, and from the chain dangled a sealed green glass tube as long as his index finger. The green glass was bubbly and spider webbed with tiny cracks, but inside the tube Lewis could glimpse something dark and metallic and pointed. Lewis unwrapped the chain and let the glass tube dangle. "This must be the Amulet of Constantine," he said. "But, Bertie, there's something else."

"What?" asked Bertie, impatience making his voice rise.

Lewis looked down at what he held. It was a delicate network of gold filigree arching over an inch-wide band of solid gold. Woven into the golden strands were glittering gems that had to be emeralds, rubies, and pearls. "I don't know for sure," said Lewis, his tone hushed, "but Bertie, I think it might be the crown of King Charles I."

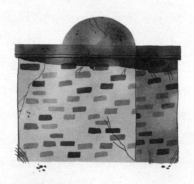

CHAPTER THIRTEEN

They did not spend much time admiring the coronet. "Which way do you think we oughta go?" asked Lewis. "Out the back of the maze, towards the house, or out the front, towards the road?"

Bertie fell silent for several moments. At last he said, "I'm sorry, Lewis. I know you'd really like to get to the road and run for help. But my mum's back in the Manor. I can't leave her. I'll go back that way." His lower lip trembled and he sniffed a couple of times. "Per-perhaps it might be better if we split up. That way old Growly could pursue only one of us."

Now that Bertie had said it, Lewis found the idea very tempting. The invisible servant had chased them twice towards the house. Like a collie herding sheep, Lewis thought. Maybe its power ended at the road, and if he could get that far, he could escape. But what about Bertie? Lewis could dream up all sorts of disasters, but this time he imagined things happening to his friend. He made up his mind. "No," he said gruffly. "We go together. Even Professor Moriarty couldn't split up Holmes and Watson—and he was lots tougher than any old spook and his invisible what's-it-called!" He hoped that he sounded much braver than he felt.

"All right," said Bertie, his tone showing his vast relief. "Towards the Manor, then. I'll take the lead out of the maze, and then up the hill as fast as we can go."

"And once we get there ..." Lewis floundered for an idea. Once they got to the Manor, then what? Climb back up his improvised rope?

What good would that do? They needed a base of operations, someplace safe. Not the toolroom in the garage—they could be trapped there if anyone came to the door, because the toolroom had only one entrance. But there *was* one room where Lewis had felt a sense of peace. "OK," he said. "Once we get to the Manor, we go to Master Martin's study to plan how to use the Amulet. Maybe we can find a book on magic there that could help us. Or maybe—this is crazy, but maybe Martin's spirit will watch out for us and keep us safe."

"Whatever you say," agreed Bertie. "As long as we don't desert my mum."

Lewis's mouth felt dry. "I guess we'd better start. I'm rested up from the dash down here, and there's no sense putting it off any longer."

Bertie led the way beneath the stone bench again. The two friends trotted quickly through the hedge maze, with Bertie's extended hand brushing the wall and providing guidance. With the Amulet hanging on its chain around his neck and the coronet clutched in his hands, Lewis thought of the nightmares that had plagued him. What if these hedges came alive suddenly? What if they wrapped their shoots around Bertie's hand and dragged him into their brushy maw? *Stop it*! he told himself. That's your trouble. You dream up calamities before they ever happen.

"Here we are," Bertie said. He halted in the entrance to the maze. "All clear?"

Lewis peered over his shoulder up the long hill towards the Manor. "Looks OK. Let's go!"

They made a run for it. At once Lewis heard a deep-throated roar, somehow *realer* than the earlier sounds had been. Bertie screamed thinly. Lewis yelled, "Run, Bertie, run!" The circular drive and safety were only ten yards away. Only five—

"*Hrr-umpf*!" Bertie had snagged his foot on something! He went sprawling, both hands thrust out to catch himself! He hit the ground with a *whump,* and his green glasses flew off his nose and dangled by one earpiece. From behind him something came dashing through the tall grass, growling and snarling!

"Get up!" screeched Lewis. His momentum had carried him a few steps past his friend. Now he stood almost on the circular drive. "Oh, gosh, Bertie, get up!"

He could *see* the course the thing took in coming up the hillside. It was already past the maze. The tall grass bent aside as the invisible pursuer bounded towards them. Clods of earth and matted grass roots flew where unseen claws ripped the ground. Bertie crouched on his hands and knees, disoriented. "Help me, Lewis!" he wailed.

Lewis ran back and grabbed Bertie's elbow. He tugged hard, but the thing had almost reached them. One more jump—

Lewis dropped Bertie's arm and grabbed the Amulet. He thrust it before him, like Professor van Helsing brandishing his crucifix at Count Dracula. The snarls became a bubbling growl of rage and frustration, and the invisible servant stopped not ten feet away. Lewis felt its hot breath and smelled its sickening stench of decay. "You stay back," he ordered the creature.

"Bertie, we're going up the hill. You got the direction?"

"Yes. Wh-what's it doing?"

"It's OK. Come on now. One step at a time."

Lewis was walking backwards. Bertie had risen to his feet. Lewis nudged him in the right direction. They took a few steps, and then he felt the asphalt of the drive underfoot. Safe! A giant depression promptly appeared in the grass just beyond the drive. The invisible servant had lain down on its belly in the grass, like a monstrous lion or tiger. Except the bent grass showed that its body was much larger than either, at least the size of a horse. Low, rumbling growls followed the boys to the Manor. Lewis did not dare pause until they had backed in the front door. Would the commotion bring Jenkins or Mrs Goodring?

Lewis knew they had to get out of the entrance hall fast.

"Can we get up to the study without going through the east wing?" he asked Bertie.

"Sure," said Bertie. "We could take the centre

stairs. That way we won't have to go anywhere close to our rooms."

Bertie led the way through the dim, darkened hallways and stairways, and they came out not far from the study. As soon as they got inside the room, they closed the door behind them. They had no way of locking it, so they sat on the floor with their backs against it. "Here we are," said Bertie. "Now what?"

Lewis hated to admit it, but he was fresh out of ideas. He had been taking everything one step at a time, and just getting to the study had been his entire goal. Now that they actually were here, he had to think of what to do. Bertie was relying on him, and maybe Cousin Pelly's and Uncle Jonathan's lives hung in the balance as well.

When he did not reply to Bertie's question right away, Bertie said, "Lewis, something is bothering me."

"What?"

"Well, old Growly can't cross the drive. At least he never has. But something got inside the

Manor to hypnotise my mum and Jenkins. What is it, and how did it get across the magic barrier?"

Lewis could answer that, because he had thought about the same question. "I'm guessing," he said, "but I *think* that somehow when we opened the vault, we brought old Witch Finder Pruitt's spirit back to the Manor. I'd bet you anything that Mr Matthew Prester of London is really a ghost—the ghost of Witch Finder Pruitt. The other thing, what we call old Growly, is Pruitt's invisible servant, the evil spirit that he controlled. I think it's more like an animal than a human being. Right now the ghost of the witch finder is using it as a kind of guard dog, probably to make sure we don't get out of the Manor and no one gets in to help us. I'll bet Martin Barnavelt made some kind of magical circle around the Manor the minute he moved back in, and that's what keeps old Growly out."

"But something got in."

"Yeah," agreed Lewis. "Remember what

Jenkins told us about Mr Prester asking if he could come inside the Manor? That's gotta be it. In the vampire stories, a vampire is a kind of evil ghost. And vampires can't come into a house until someone living inside invites them. Jenkins didn't mean to do it, but when he told Mr Prester to go into the Manor, he broke the protective spell that Martin put around the house. The ghost got inside, and that's how he got a chance to hypnotise your mum and Jenkins, and to kidnap my uncle and Cousin Pelly."

"D-do you think we can fight something like that?" faltered Bertie.

"I don't know, Bertie. Maybe this thing will help. I wonder what it is." He held up the bubbly, cracked, green glass tube, but he could not clearly make out what it held inside. He dropped the Amulet down inside the front of his shirt. Somehow its presence near his heart comforted him. He had put the coronet down beside him. Now he rose to his feet and picked it up. "Let's hide this crown and see if we can find anything in any of these books that might help."

One of the dustcovers concealed an enormous old desk of some heavy, dark wood. Lewis opened the drawers and found a deep one that was empty. He slipped the coronet down into that, closed the drawer, and rearranged the cover. Then as Bertie kept guard at the door, Lewis began to look at the rows and rows of books. He found lots of things that ordinarily might have made him pause: A Second Folio of Shakespeare's plays, a French translation of the *Necronomicon* by someone named Abdul Alhazred, and a slim volume called *The Lore of Model Railroading*. He found cookbooks and poetry collections, mystery novels and arithmetic books, accounts of piracy and collections of stories about dragons. But he found nothing that promised to help him understand the magic of the Amulet or to give him any ideas about how to combat a sorcerer's ghost. He did not give up, but went on to the next set of shelves.

Most of the day passed in this way. Bertie complained once that he was hungry. Lewis felt ravenous too, but he did not dare try to sneak down to the kitchen for something to eat. "We just have to live with it," he said, sighing. Bertie must have agreed, because he did not bring up the subject of food again.

The problem was that the library held so many books. Worse, they were in no order at all—unless you counted the order of size. The folios, which are larger books, were on the taller shelves, the middle-sized quartos and octavos on the shorter shelves, and the even smaller sixteen mos and thirty-two mos were crammed into shelves only a few inches apart. However, since size does not determine content, books jostled each other with no sense or order. Lewis found a biography of Izaak Walton, the world's most famous fisherman, wedged between a tome of wedding etiquette and a fat travel guide to scenic Luxembourg. Searching for one particular book in all this confusion was worse than looking for a needle in a haystack. It was more like looking for one particular needle in a needle factory.

Outside, the sun sank low and shadows stretched out long and black across the lawn. Lewis had to drag a heavy chair around with him to be able to look at the books on the higher shelves, and that made the going even slower. He felt more and more frustrated as he prowled through all the useless books. He wondered why Cousin Pelly didn't simply sell some of these volumes if he needed money. Lewis was no expert, but he knew that some of the books were very old and probably very valuable. He was almost sure, for example, that the big black Gutenberg Bible would bring a high price. But maybe the books had sentimental value, like the big cardboard suitcase that he and Jonathan had decided not to take on their holiday because it was in such bad shape. Still, Lewis would never have thrown it away. The suitcase had belonged to his father, and it was special to him.

The light faded to dusk, and finally Lewis

finished the last set of shelves. "Nothing," he reported in a gloomy voice. He felt grimy and exhausted. A fine film of book dust covered his face and hands and made his eyes feel scratchy. "I guess if Martin Barnavelt had any volumes of magic, he must have hidden them. And no, I don't want to search for secret bookshelves. Bertie, I hate to say it, but I think we'd better try to get away from the Manor. The sun is setting, and I don't wanna be here after dark."

"I shall stay," said Bertie at once.

Lewis grimaced. "OK, OK," he muttered. "But we gotta get some food. You stay here, and I'll sneak down and grab us something. If I'm not back in ten minutes, you'll know that you should try to escape."

"No," said Bertie. "We go together, or not at all."

"Oh, all right." Lewis tried to sound cross, but what he felt was immense relief. He did not look forward to creeping through those dark hallways.

They opened the study door, and Lewis looked

out. Nothing. Together he and Bertie stepped into the hall and headed for the stairway.

Slam! The door crashed shut behind them with a sound like a gunshot. Both boys yelled in fright. Lewis spun in the sudden darkness and saw an eerie glow behind him. It hovered, shapeless and uncertain at first, a greenish-blue vapoury-looking mist about the size of a man. Then almost immediately it took on shape and form. Lewis recognised the black-clothed man he had glimpsed down by the gatekeeper's cottage! The face was long and lean, with a high forehead and deep-set, glaring eyes. The lips split apart, and the apparition gave Lewis a horrifying snaggle-toothed grin, just like the evil leer he had seen on the face of the moon.

"At last!" Did Lewis hear the words, or did they sound only in his mind? He couldn't tell. The sound, or the feeling, made him dizzy and breathless. He felt the way he had in the awful nightmares, when he tried to run but could hardly move a muscle. "The last of the accursed Barnavelts, in my hands after all this great while! I tell thee, I have waited nearly three hundred years for my vengeance. And now 'tis mine at last! I hold thee my prisoner, thou accursed whelp!"

"Run!" screamed Bertie, and that broke the dreadful spell. Lewis screamed too, and he spun on his heel. He and Bertie pelted down the dark hallway—

They ran right into a tall figure. Bony hands clamped on to the boys' shoulders. Lewis thought his heart would burst from fear. He heard mocking laughter.

Then the electric lights flickered on, dim and orange and ghastly. Lewis could see his captor now. Cousin Pelly stood gripping Lewis and Bertie, his face turned down towards them.

But his expression, like Mrs Goodring's and Jenkins's, was empty and mindless. The ghost of the witch finder had somehow enslaved poor old Pelly. And now Bertie and Lewis were in the evil ghost's power.

CHAPTER FOURTEEN

Down, down, down. Unspeaking, moving like a robot, Cousin Pelly forced the boys to climb down a winding circular staircase. "Where are we going?" Lewis asked, but his relative did not reply.

"I don't know," said Bertie. He had thought the question was for him. "Was that a trapdoor we went through?"

"Yeah," replied Lewis. "It's under a rug in the middle of the front-hall floor."

"I didn't even know it was there," said Bertie.

The bony hands gave them a shake, and the boys fell silent. The circular stairs twisted downwards through a stone-walled shaft, with dim and flickering light coming from candles stuck into sconces every few steps. The air felt damp and smelled musty, as if the place had been closed off for ages. Finally they reached the bottom of the stairs. Ahead of them loomed a tall, arched door of oak. Pelly shoved them roughly towards this, and it swung slowly open as they approached, although no hand touched it.

Lewis gasped. Now he knew where they were. The room beyond the door rose to a barrel-arched ceiling. The floor was glistening stone, blackened with age and slippery with moisture. A long table had been set up at the far end. It held a brass candelabrum with four tapers burning in it, giving the dismal room the dimmest possible illumination. And thanks to the uncertain light, Lewis could see a miserable figure standing in a kind of waist-high wooden cage to the left of the table. It was his uncle

Jonathan, still in his carrot-coloured pyjamas and nightcap, with his hands chained in front of him.

Lewis glared wildly around. Shapes stood in the dark shadowy corners of the room, shapes that could be tables or chests or other odds and ends of furniture. Only they weren't. Without even being able to see them clearly, Lewis knew that they were instruments of torture. This was the abandoned wine cellar that Witch Finder Pruitt had made his headquarters. This was where he tormented and wrung confessions from his hapless victims. This was the courtroom where he had held his trials for witchcraft.

"The prisoners will be placed in the dock."

Lewis jerked his gaze back to the table. No one had sat behind it before, but now he saw a tall chair, and in it a spectral form. Old Witch Finder Pruitt, or his ghost, sat there, his bald dome hidden under an elaborate wig. He wore the long black robes of a British judge. Pelly pushed the boys forward, forcing them into the waist-high cage where Uncle Jonathan stood. "Hello, boys," he said, his voice sad and weary. "Lewis, I'm sorry I got you into this mess."

Despite all his fear and dread, Lewis felt like hugging Jonathan. "Gosh, Uncle Jonathan, it's all my fault—"

"Silence!"

Bertie gasped in fear. Lewis flinched and looked back at the apparition behind the table. It looked different, somehow. Then he realised that the features of the witch finder were changing from moment to moment. They wavered and swam, like a face seen through a windowpane with rain wriggling down over it. One instant the face was the stern and cunning countenance of a man in hearty middle age. The next the cheeks and eyes had sunken, the hair had withered away from the temples, and the mouth had gone gap-toothed and slack. It was as if Pruitt were aging from forty-five to a hundred and then going back again, over and over.

"The other prisoner will enter the dock."

Pelly walked stiffly into the now-crowded cage.

"Mr Barnavelt," whispered Bertie. "Please, sir, snap out of it!"

Pelly did not respond. He stood staring blindly ahead, his arms slack at his sides. Lewis thought desperately of running away, but the moment the thought entered his mind, the door swung closed with a *boom*, making him start violently. No escape that way.

The ghost at the table spoke again: "Prisoners at the bar, three of ye stand accused of the most horrible and vile crime of sorcery. Ye are descended from that accursed warlock Martin Barnavelt, who did foully enchant me in my days of life and cut short my good work. How do ye plead?"

Pelly said nothing, and Lewis was too frightened to speak. But Jonathan raised his voice and boomed, "Not guilty, your dishonour!"

The ghost continued as if it had not heard: "The fourth prisoner is a willing accomplice to the crimes of the others. He shall be judged as harshly, and delivered to the same punishment as they. The trial will proceed."

"You're no judge," said Jonathan in an angry voice. "And this is no trial. You were the evil sorcerer, and you know it. Martin Barnavelt never hurt anyone in his life except you, and you asked for it!"

"We who do the work of good must sometimes employ the methods of the doers of evil," the ghost said. "True, I did learn the ways and wiles of sorcery. But that was to entrap the witches that did bedevil our land, and to prolong my days upon the earth, that they might be caught and punished!"

Jonathan snorted. To Lewis and Bertie, he said, "Don't believe the old liar. Malachiah Pruitt traded his soul for control of an evil spirit. It prolonged his days, all right—he didn't age at all for fifty years. But when Martin Barnavelt banished the spirit, all of old Pruitt's evil fell on his shoulders, and the shock turned him into a doddering old man before it killed him!"

"You *know* about Martin Barnavelt and his magic?" asked Lewis, amazed.

"He was my ancestor, and yours too, Lewis. Sure, I know all about Martin Barnavelt. Maybe Pelly thought all the old family stories were just fairy tales, but I knew better. Martin Barnavelt studied magic, all right, but he never used it for evil. And the worst day that he ever lived, he was twice as good a man as the wicked witch finder ever was!" The words sounded contemptuous and brave, but Lewis could see a worried light in his uncle's eyes.

"That will change, thou miscreant," said the ghost. "Thy foolish nephew released the phantom that served me. It summoned my own spirit from its slumber, and allowed me to walk again upon the earth. I spelled the inhabitants of the Manor to be my slaves and follow my will, and they released to me the trunk containing my magical supplies. The sacrifice of a few chickens strengthened me to use those supplies. And when thou and thy sorcerous kin are dead, then I shall walk the earth as flesh and blood again, free to find all wickedness and to punish it!"

"What do you mean?" demanded Jonathan. "You don't have any jurisdiction over me or my relatives!"

The apparition laughed in a nasty way. "I have the jurisdiction of the righteous!" it howled. "Behold! Through the mystical knowledge I gained in my long studies, I know a most secret and cunning spell. One by one, ye miscreants will roast at the stake for thy sins! And as the life burns from each of ye, I shall gain new life! This ghostly form shall gain flesh and blood, and I shall be man alive again, fit to cleanse this sinful world. And this time I shall succeed, and claim rulership of England—of the whole world!"

"You're crazy, Pruitt," growled Jonathan.

"Which shall be first?" murmured the ghost. "The eldest? The youngest? Shall I give thee a taste of thy doom, thou bearded warlock?" The wavering spirit began to chant weird words.

In the dock beside Lewis, Jonathan stiffened. "What's wrong, Uncle Jonathan?" asked Lewis.

His uncle did not reply. Sweat beaded on his forehead, and his eyes squeezed shut in pain. His teeth clenched, and a groan forced its way out. Then the ghost's chanting stopped, and Jonathan staggered. "Whew!" he breathed.

"What's wrong?" squeaked Bertie.

Jonathan shook his head. "An illusion spell. That flickering phantom had me believing I was lying on a rack, with my arms and my legs being stretched out of their sockets. And I fell for it!"

Lewis looked at the ghost. Was it a little more solid? Did its features change more slowly from middle age to decrepitude? He thought they did.

"Thou starest at me?" grinned the spook. "Then sample thy fate, young warlock!" Again the ghost chanted.

Lewis gasped. The underground dungeon faded away.

He was standing in a walled courtyard. His arms had been tied behind him, around a post almost as thick as a telegraph pole. And he stood on a jumbled mound of split logs, reeking of pine resin and oak sap. The spirit of the witch finder planned to burn him at the stake!

The moment the thought came to him, Lewis heard the dreadful crackle of fire. He screamed for help, and his shout echoed back at him from the stone walls. Wisps of smoke floated up. Then the smoke grew thicker, ragged and grey. Waves of heat swept up from the wood, choking Lewis. Tears streamed from his eyes. He felt a searing lick of flame blistering his legs—

And then the chanting stopped, and he was standing back in the dock. He swayed and gasped. Even the hot, stagnant air seemed cool by comparison with his vivid hallucination. And this time he was sure of it: old Witch Finder Pruitt *was* more solid, less transparent, than he had been. He lives on other people's pain and fear, Lewis thought confusedly. They make him stronger and more real. And death makes him strongest of all! He vaguely heard his uncle asking, "Lewis? Are you all right?"

An idea came to Lewis then. He was crying, but he forced himself to speak boldly: "Yeah, you may burn us all to crisps and become real again. But if you plan to rule the world, you're gonna need a crown. And you don't have one, because my ancestor took it away from you. And you know what? I hid it where you'll never find it, not in a million years!"

"What!" thundered the ghost. "Thou hast my crown? I demand it of thee, insolent whelp!"

"Go soak your head," said Lewis.

The ghost's expression became cagey. "Boy, tell me where thou hast concealed my crown. Do it, and perhaps I shall let thee live. Perhaps I shall even adopt thee as my son—teach thee the words of command over spirits, that thou shalt be a mighty man of power. "

Lewis blinked. He had not thought of that possibility. Although Jonathan fooled around with white magic, Lewis had always been frightened to try anything like that. He had been frightened of people and things all his life, he realised. For a moment he imagined himself wielding sorcerous power. He could turn all the bullies at school into frogs and mice. He could be so powerful that nothing could ever hurt him, and never again would he have to be afraid or dream up disasters that might happen to him.

But then hot anger flooded over him. What would be the price of such power? The life of eccentric, likeable old Cousin Pelly? Of his loyal friend Bertie? Of kind and gentle Uncle Jonathan?

"No deal," he said. "But here's what I will do: if you'll let us go, I'll get the crown for you. How's that?"

Greed and wrath warred in the ghostly face. A sly look replaced them. "Give us the coronet first," the spirit purred. "And then we shall consider what leniency we shall offer thee."

"Lewis, no," Bertie cried. "He's trying to trick you."

Lewis ignored his friend. "OK, I'll do it," he said. "You'll have to let me go get it, though."

"My slave shall go with thee."

Lewis looked up at Jonathan and gave him a wink. Jonathan looked startled for a moment. But he raised no objection when Lewis stepped out of the dock. Lewis walked to the door. It swung open at his approach. All the way back to the study, Cousin Pelly plodded right along behind him. He had no chance to make a break for it.

But Lewis had no plans to run away. In the study he reached down to the drawer where he had hidden the crown. He busied himself doing something to it for a moment, and then he straightened. He walked past Pelly and downstairs again, with his hypnotised old relative trudging along right behind him. Down he went again, down that spiral staircase to the horribly gruesome underground chamber.

The scene had not changed. Jonathan and Bertie still cowered in the dock. The wavering form of Witch Finder Pruitt still shimmered behind the table. Its eyes glowed a hungry red the second Lewis entered with the coronet. "Mine!" screeched the spectral creature. "Mine!

The just rewards of my diligence and cleverness, stolen from me by your ancestor! Approach, boy! Crown me King of England—of the world!"

Lewis licked his lips. He hated to draw near the eerie creature, but he had to do it. He edged around the table. He stood beside the high-backed chair. "Crown me!" the spirit ordered again.

He can't pick it up, Lewis realised. The ghost might have the power to materialise, and it might even be solid enough for the crown to sit on its head and not sink through like a spoon sliding into jelly. But it wasn't real enough to grasp material objects. That was why it had entranced Jenkins and Mrs Goodring and Cousin Pelly. The most it could do was float trunks downstairs or make doors open and close by themselves. Lewis raised the coronet and held it over the ghost's head. The judge's wig faded and vanished, leaving the patchy, bald head of Witch Finder Pruitt exposed. Slowly, Lewis lowered the crown into place. It settled on to the ghost's head. Both of Lewis's hands felt cold, as if he had stuck them into the icebox.

"Ha!" exclaimed the ghost. "What is rightfully mine has been returned. Now, foolish boy, thou shalt die—thou and all thine accursed kin!"

"Yeah?" shouted Lewis. "You sure you can pull that off? What if you're wearing the Amulet of Constantine around your stupid head?"

"*What*!" the ghost shrieked. Lewis had wound the chain of the Amulet around the crown again, just as he had found it, and he had tucked the Amulet into the network of gold filigree among the emeralds and rubies. Now the glass tube suddenly dropped free and dangled on its chain right between Witch Finder Pruitt's hollow eyes.

"Attaboy, Lewis!" yelled Jonathan, and immediately he began to chant something.

The glass tube lit up with a supernatural glow. The ghost of the witch finder leaped out of its seat, clawing at the crown. But the coronet had frozen itself to his skull. The ghost rose into the air, whirled, screamed, and

screeched, and all the time the Amulet shone brighter and brighter. In its green glow an alarming change flowed over Pruitt's features: he grew older by the second. He looked a hundred years old. Then he was like a living mummy, with his skin stretched horribly over his bones, so tight that it split and peeled away. His teeth showed in a grimace. The lips and gums shrank away from them until they were bare, yellow, and dry. The witch finder became a rattling skeleton, his black judge's robe flanking away to nothing. And then Jonathan's chanting voice rose in a mighty crescendo. The Amulet gave a final, brilliant flash. In its unearthly light, Lewis saw the writhing skeleton silently explode into a cloud of grey dust—

And the coronet fell from empty air to clatter on the table. Lewis snatched it up in the sudden darkness. He heard the clink and clank of chains. "What happened? What happened?" bawled Bertie.

"Lewis just saved our hides!" yelled Jonathan.

"The chains have dropped away from my wrists and ankles. You did it, Lewis! The Amulet sent old Witch Finder Pruitt back to the grave! We're free!"

CHAPTER FIFTEEN

"You bring the crown and the Amulet, Lewis,"
Jonathan said. "Cousin Pelly has fainted. I'll
have to carry him upstairs."

They hurried up the winding staircase. Lewis
and Bertie heaved the heavy lid of the trapdoor
over, and it closed with a bang. They found
Jenkins slumped in the downstairs hallway,
unconscious, and Mrs Goodring in a dead faint
outside Lewis's door, where she must have been
standing all day. Lewis put the crown and
Amulet down as he and Jonathan rubbed her

hands. She did not respond, and Bertie, who stood a little apart from them, began to sob.

Just then someone knocked at the door downstairs. The hollow thuds of the knocker echoed through the big old house. "Get that, Lewis," Jonathan said as he picked up Mrs Goodring. He began to carry her downstairs as Lewis ran ahead. The knocking continued.

Lewis threw the door open. A middle-aged man stood in the light flowing out from the open door. He wore a baggy brown jacket and a rumpled tie, and he carried a brown bowler hat in his hands. He was the image of Inspector Lestrade, the bumbling policeman in the Sherlock Holmes stories. "I beg your pardon," he said. "I'm Sergeant Norman Spiney, from the village. A few minutes ago we received a rather odd call from one of my colleagues in London, a Constable Dwiggins. He seemed to believe that something might be wrong here."

Lewis didn't know what to say, but Jonathan came up behind him. "You're a policeman? Did you come in a police car?"

The sergeant blinked in confusion. "I did, but it's at the foot of the drive. A chain—"

Jonathan ignored his explanation and said, "Good! You can help me get these people to a doctor. They're all unconscious."

"What?" asked Spiney, staring unbelievingly at this big, red-bearded man in the loud orange pyjamas.

"Help me!" barked Jonathan. "Bring your car up and carry these people out to it while I get dressed!"

Lewis went down the drive to help Sergeant Spiney loosen the chain. He heard no grunts, no growls, no sound at all from the invisible servant. From the fresh, clean feel of the air, Lewis guessed the evil spirit had vanished along with its wicked master. After some moments of fumbling in the dark, the two of them managed to lower the chain. The sergeant drove his police car up to the front door of the Manor.

They got Mrs Goodring and Jenkins into the front seat, beside Spiney, and Cousin Pelly into the back. Spiney looked a little unhappy at the overcrowding. "Perhaps you and these young gentlemen might remain here—" he started.

"Not on your life!" Jonathan snapped. "Pile in, boys!"

They crowded into the back seat. Cousin Pelly lolled like a rag doll against one door. Bertie squeezed in against the other. Uncle Jonathan sat in the middle, and Lewis sat on his lap. Ordinarily he would have been embarrassed by this, but now he felt comfortable and safe.

Sergeant Spiney sped towards the village of Dinsdale with the odd British siren yelping away: *HOO-hah, HOO-hah, HOO-hah*! it seemed to cry. Dinsdale had no real hospital, but it did have a clinic, and the doctor there put all three patients to bed. The sergeant spoke with Jonathan at some length, and he came away with the impression that a gas leak or something of that sort had knocked out the victims. As no crime seemed to have been committed, he satisfied himself with that.

Bertie collapsed from nervous exhaustion, and the doctor put him to bed too. Jonathan and Lewis waited in the small room as the doctor treated his patients. "That was good thinking, Lewis," Jonathan said, putting his hand on Lewis's shoulder. "You saved us all."

"But I got us all into trouble first," admitted Lewis. He told Jonathan the whole story then, from start to finish. His uncle listened patiently and sympathetically. By the time Lewis finished the tale, he was crying. "So if I hadn't been fooling around like that, the evil spirit would never have been released," he sobbed.

In a gentle voice, Jonathan said, "Why didn't you tell me any of this before?"

Lewis shook his head. "I was afraid to. I acted so dumb. And I kept thinking what would happen if you got mad and kicked me out."

"Kicked you out?" Jonathan sounded truly astonished.

"Uh-huh. I was a-afraid that y-you would be so mad that you wouldn't want me to live with you any more."

Jonathan shook his head. Then he sighed. "This is my fault."

Lewis blinked at him through his tears. "What?"

Jonathan shrugged. "Well, I'm just an old bachelor. A girl I was in love with jilted me and broke my heart thirty years ago, so I never married. And so I never had children of my own and never learned how to talk to kids. If I'd behaved the way I should, I would have listened to you more—"

"But I caused all the trouble," Lewis insisted. "Gosh, Uncle Jonathan, *you* didn't do anything wrong. You've been swell to me, and I lo—I mean, I—I—"

Jonathan held his arms open, and Lewis hugged him. Softly, Jonathan said, "Tell me whenever you're ready, Lewis. And I love you too." He fished a handkerchief out of his pocket, and Lewis blew his nose.

After a moment Lewis said, "Do you think we got rid of the ghost? For good, I mean?"

"I sure do," said Jonathan. "But we'll ask Mrs Zimmermann. about it when we get back to America. She'll know all about this lucky charm." He pulled the Amulet of Constantine from his vest pocket. "We'll give the crown to Cousin Pelly, but I think we'd better hold on to this little item for safekeeping."

A few minutes later the doctor came and said that everyone was awake again. Awake but confused. Jonathan and Lewis went to see Cousin Pelly, who appeared dazed. "Oh, there you are," he murmured. "Dashed odd, but I seem to have lost my memory. Last thing I can recall is a terrible storm and a big flash of lightning. Was I struck, or what?"

The others had had a similar lapse of memory. In the morning they were all ready to go home again, but before they did, Lewis and Jonathan had a talk with Bertie. They all agreed not to mention the story of the evil spirit and the ghost. If Jenkins, Mrs Goodring, and Cousin Pelly did not recall the horrible ordeal, so much the better.

Uncle Jonathan hired a car, and he drove them to Barnavelt Manor, although he had some trouble adjusting to the right-hand drive. The first thing he did upon arriving was to inspect the gatehouse. He emerged after some minutes. "Mr Prester left a note," he told Pelly. "He says he feels much better and is returning to London. I took the liberty of burning some, ah, trash that he left behind in an old trunk." Lewis noticed smoke coming from the chimney. He guessed that Jonathan had destroyed whatever magical papers and implements the ghost of Pruitt had used in his dire spells.

At the Manor itself Jonathan, Bertie, and Lewis made the other three comfortable around the dining-room table. Then Jonathan went upstairs for a moment. When he came back down, he brought the jewelled crown with him. "Cousin Pelly," he said, "Lewis and Bertie have been playing detective, and they uncovered this fancy hat. Since they found it on your property, I'd say it belongs to you."

Pelly's grey eyes nearly bulged out of his head. "I say! That looks—rather expensive!"

That afternoon he and Jonathan went into the village, where Pelly knew an antiques and valuables dealer. When they returned, Pelly was exultant. "This could be the answer to all my problems!" he said. "It's worth heaps of money, simply heaps! I could open up the rest of the Manor, and repair the west wing, and—" He broke off. "But of course it isn't really mine," he said. "Bertie found it, and finders keepers."

"No, sir," objected Mrs Goodring, her voice indignant. They argued back and forth for one whole day, each trying to give the crown to the other. Finally Jonathan proposed a truce.

"If this dazzling derby is really the crown of Charles I, it may not belong to either one of you," he pointed out. "But if you get to keep it, why not simply split the proceeds fifty-fifty? If the fellow who appraised it is right, even half of its value should be a big enough fortune for anybody!"

And so they left it at that. Pelly hired a lawyer—only he called it a solicitor—to determine whether he could actually claim the crown or would have to settle for only a reward. The lawyer, a shrewd-looking little fellow, thought Pelly stood a good chance of keeping the coronet for himself. "Possession is nine-tenths of the law, you know," he advised. "And since your family have had possession for nearly three hundred years, that should account for the other tenth. However, we shall see what we shall see."

Soon after that Jonathan and Lewis took the train back to London. They dropped in on Constable Dwiggins, who had been told the story that Sergeant Spiney had settled on: a gas leak had overcome the adults in the Manor, and the boys had not known what to do to help. He apologised for the delay in calling Sergeant Spiney, but as he explained, "My mum is getting forgetful, and night had fallen before she remembered your message. When I couldn't get through to the Manor, I phoned the Dinsdale police station and spoke to Sergeant Spiney, and the rest is history."

"Thanks," said Lewis with a grin.

"Think nothing of it. But that was jolly good work on your part, Mr Holmes," said Dwiggins with a wink at Lewis. "And always call upon the Metropolitan Police for a bit of help when you find yourself in a tight spot!"

That afternoon Jonathan and Lewis boarded a plane and flew back to New York. They returned to New Zebedee on a hot, still Monday in the summer, and Mrs Zimmermann and Rose Rita met them at the bus stop in front of Heemsoth's Rexall Drug Store. Mrs Zimmermann wore a purple-flowered summer dress, and she gave them a wonderful, wrinkly smile of a welcome. Rose Rita had got rid of the cast on her ankle and was ready to take on Lewis in a race. The four friends went to Mrs Zimmermann's lake cottage for a picnic, but Lewis and Jonathan did not talk about their adventure. Both had been too shaken to feel comfortable discussing it so soon.

However, Mrs Zimmermann and Rose Rita told them an astounding story. While Lewis and his uncle had been away, Mrs Zimmermann and Rose Rita had taken a little trip of their own. It sounded frightening and exhilarating, because they had somehow travelled far back into the past, and when they had returned, Mrs Zimmermann had found a way to recover her lost magical powers. So they had a lot to celebrate.

School began the day after Labour Day, and Lewis discovered that the other kids noticed a change in him. Occasionally one of the popular boys, Dizzy Shelmacher or Beanie Inquist, would pick Lewis when choosing up sides for a baseball game. True, they usually picked him at the end of the roster. He also had to play right field, where he almost never had a chance to catch a ball or make a play. Still, for the first time Lewis was playing baseball, just like a regular boy. He did his best and developed an unexpected talent for bunting runners from first to second. Sometimes he even reached first base. Since that meant he had to run as fast as he could, Lewis worked to keep the extra pounds off, and he was successful. However, he still had no interest in other boys chasing him and throwing him to the ground, so he did not play football after baseball season ended. He could always wait for spring.

At the beginning of October, he finally felt brave enough to tell Rose Rita about the mysterious vault, the invisible servant, and the witch finder. Rose Rita was full of admiration for the way he had handled things. "You're getting to be a regular Philip Marlowe," she said. Philip Marlowe was the hero of one of the detective shows Rose Rita listened to on the radio. He was a tough guy, and Lewis fairly glowed at the comparison.

Jonathan also told Mrs Zimmermann the story of their adventure. When he showed the Amulet to her, Mrs Zimmermann let out a low whistle. "Know what you've got, Brush Mush?"

"I know it's powerful enough to knock an evil ghost loopy," said Jonathan with a grin. "But you're the amulets expert, Haggy. You know what this doohickey is, so give!"

Mrs Zimmermann explained that the metallic shape inside the glass tube was a nail from the True Cross. "It's a relic that dates back to the Roman Emperor Constantine," she said. "After some centuries in Rome, it wound up in the Holy Land. Then the Crusaders came, and it disappeared. I guess one of your ancestors was a knight in shining iron britches who rode to Jerusalem and came back with it. Lucky for you he did, because a good magician who wields this calls on a great power that can banish the most evil foes."

"It's all yours, Haggy," said Jonathan. "And it's a relief to get it off my hands. It may be heap big magic, but I'm really just a parlour magician, and using it once was enough for me."

Rose Rita said, "Something's bothering me. If Nasty Pruitt hypnotised Cousin Pelham and Mrs Goodring and Jenkins, why didn't he do the same thing to the other three?"

Mrs Zimmermann smiled. "I think there are two reasons," she said thoughtfully. "First, Bertie can't see, and I suspect that Pruitt had to look his victims in the eyes for his evil spell to work. Second, both Frazzle Face and Lewis are descended from a good magician. Cousin

Pelham is too, but he didn't believe in his great-umpty-great-grandfather Martin's magic, and both Jonathan and Lewis did. When you know and trust it, good magic has a way of protecting you even if no one speaks a spell or waves a wand. Of course I could be wrong, but with the wacky witch finder out of the picture, it really doesn't matter."

"Do you think the spirit of old Pruitt is gone for good?" Lewis asked Mrs Zimmermann.

Mrs Zimmermann winked. "Gone for good, banished to the outer darkness, and sent packing—and his invisible servant with him!" She sighed. "Isn't it funny how some of the people who think they are doing the most good cause the most trouble?"

"I don't think Malachiah Pruitt believed he was doing good," said Rose Rita. "He was just an evil old man who hated everyone."

"Well, he's gone now, and he will never be back, so we don't have to worry about him any more," said Jonathan firmly, and that ended the discussion.

Several times that autumn Lewis received letters from Bertie. Of course, Bertie had dictated the letters to his mother, and she wrote them out in her beautiful old-fashioned copperplate handwriting. Lewis was always glad to hear from Bertie, and he answered the letters promptly. Unfortunately, Bertie reported, Cousin Pelly was having difficulty in disposing of the coronet. Not even the experts really knew if it had belonged to Charles I. It certainly was not the official state crown, but many of Charles's other valuables had vanished during the war, and the records of them had also disappeared. It looked like the legal questions could last for months.

Halloween arrived, and then Thanksgiving, and at last Christmas. Mrs Zimmermann baked heaps of cakes and pies and cookies, and on 21st December Jonathan and Lewis went out and cut a huge Christmas tree. Rose Rita and Mrs Zimmermann came over to help decorate it. Jonathan hung all the usual ornaments on the higher branches, and Rose Rita and Lewis took care of the lower ones. They draped yards of garlands and tossed strings of tinsel. Mrs Zimmerman worked a little magic, and the Christmas lights crept out of their boxes and strung themselves on the tree. Then when Jonathan plugged them in, they twinkled in a thousand different colours. Each bulb would shine in one colour, like red or green or blue, and then immediately shimmer to a whole different hue, white or yellow or violet. And every so often, all the lights would flash purple at the same time. "Quite a show, Frizzy Wig," Jonathan complimented.

"Why, thank you, Weird Beard," said Mrs Zimmermann with a smile. "Now, who's for some chocolate layer cake and milk?"

While they were having their cake, they heard the mail slot flap open in the hallway. "I'll get it," said Lewis. He hurried out. A few envelopes lay on the hall floor. There were some letters for Jonathan, an electric bill, and a square envelope addressed to Lewis, in a child's awkward printing. The postmark showed it came from New York.

Lewis frowned. Who could be sending him a card from New York? Inside the envelope was a hand-drawn and coloured card that looked like the work of a six-year-old. The front showed two crudely sketched figures in front of a Christmas tree. One wore a deerstalker hat and stood beside a fireplace, and the other lay in a hospital bed and had a moustache. The message underneath the figures read, "What do I wish you, my dear Holmes?"

Lewis grinned as he opened the card. Inside, in rainbow colours, was the message, "Elementary! A Merry Christmas!" And the signature read, "Bertie 'Watson' Goodring."

"He can see," breathed Lewis. "He can see!"

"What came?" Jonathan called from the study.

"The best Christmas present ever!" Lewis yelled at the top of his lungs. And he ran to show the others the wonderful card.

The End

John Bellairs (1938–1991) was an award-winning American author of many gothic mystery novels for children and young adults, including *The House With a Clock in Its Walls*, which received both the New York Times Outstanding Book of the Year Award and the American Library Association Children's Books of International Interest Award, *The Lamp from the Warlock's Tomb*, which won the Edgar Award and *The Spectre from the Magician's Museum*, which won the New York Public Library 'Best Books for Teen Age' Award.

Brad Strickland has written more than eighty-five published books, including entries in the Lewis Barnavelt and Johnny Dixon series, following the death of the original series creator, John Bellairs. He is a Professor Emeritus of English and lives in Georgia with his wife, Barbara.

Have you read the previous book?

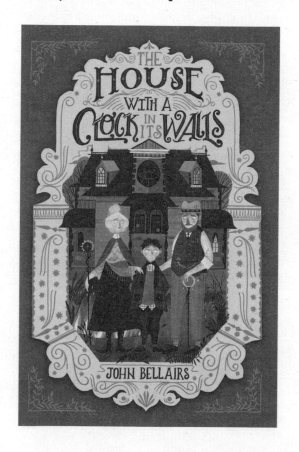

Have you read the previous book?

Piccadilly
PRESS

Have you read the previous book?

Piccadilly
PRESS

Have you read the previous book?

Piccadilly
PRESS

Look out for more magic from
Lewis and Rose Rita

THE DOOM OF THE HAUNTED OPERA

When Lewis and Rose Rita explore an abandoned theatre, they discover an unpublished opera score called 'The Day of Doom'. Little do they know that the opera was composed to awaken the dead and enslave the world. Can Lewis and Rose Rita stop the dead from coming back to life?

Coming in 2019

Piccadilly
PRESS

Thank you for choosing a Piccadilly Press book.

If you would like to know more about our
authors, our books or if you'd just like to know
what we're up to, you can find us online.

www.piccadillypress.co.uk

And you can also find us on:

We hope to see you soon!